It-Girl and Other Stories

AMY KRISTOFF

Deer Run Press
Cushing, Maine

Copyright © 2022 Amy Kristoff.

All rights reserved. No part this book may be reproduced or transmitted in any form or by any means, electronic or mechanical, including photocopying, recording, or by any information storage and retrieval system, without written permission from the copyright owner.

This is a work of fiction. Names, characters, places and incidents either are the product of the author's imagination or are used fictitiously, and any resemblance to any actual persons (living or dead), events, or locales is entirely coincidental.

Library of Congress Card Number: 2022946452

ISBN: 978-1-937869-16-8

First Printing, 2022

Published by
Deer Run Press
8 Cushing Road
Cushing, ME 04563

Contents

It-Girl//1

Who Says Real Estate Is Boring?//34

Who Is the Selfish One?//54

Dead Wait//71

End of the Road//84

All in the Family//93

Next of Kin//114

It-Girl

Alicia Bellcamp worked at Brewer Insurance Company on Main Street (also known as Route 36) in Clearview, Michigan, a town of about ten-thousand people, 75 miles southwest of Detroit. She lived in a small, white vinyl-sided, A-frame house located about two miles from the office.

The neighborhood was seemingly worlds away from the non-stop bustle of Route 36. The two-lane highway was a popular road for truckers if they wanted a short-cut to the north-south routes that were in the middle of the state.

Alicia had moved to Clearview from the St. Louis area and shortly after doing so, there was a terrible accident on Route 36 in late October, around two a.m. It had snowed a little and the pavement was slippery, as the Highway Department hadn't gotten around to doing anything. Four lives were lost in the collision involving a loaded semi-trailer and two cars. Alicia didn't pay close attention to all the details because the incident struck too close to home, having lost her husband, Troy, and daughter, Claudia, in an auto accident almost three years earlier.

Formerly Alicia taught sixth through eighth-grade English in a suburban St. Louis school district. Troy taught ninth and tenth-grade math over the state line, in the Belleville, Illinois school district. He had a much longer commute, but he liked to drive, ironically enough.

People around Clearview talked about "The Dangers of Route Thirty-six" from that day on, as if it there was some sort of jinx. Alicia didn't appreciate hearing that kind of thing. She was a bit superstitious as it was, and she was even more so after losing the two most important people in her life. It seemed like anymore she lived, waiting for the other shoe to drop, so to speak.

Alicia's life completely changed the day she lost her husband and their only child. She still felt guilty for not being with them when they flew to California on Troy's and Claudia's spring break. Claudia had attended a parochial school, and her break happened to coincide with the Belleville school district's, not the one in which Alicia taught.

Continuing to teach after Troy's and Claudia's deaths was entirely unthinkable. Alicia gave notice she would be quitting once school was out for the summer. Hanging on until then was nearly unbearable, but it was imperative she stay busy.

It never rains in California? Alicia didn't think so either until it rained and rained (and rained) when Troy and Claudia flew to Pasadena to visit his mother, Eleanor, who still lived in the same house he grew up in. They'd rented a car, so Troy could show Claudia all the places he went as a kid. Who could have guessed they'd never return? It was all thanks to Troy's success in avoiding having the rental car hit head on by a drunk driver. Troy steered the car to the shoulder and slowed down but nicked the guardrail with the right front bumper. Meanwhile the oncoming vehicle continued to bear down on the rental car, so Troy accelerated again. However, in all the commotion, he apparently forgot to turn the car back toward the lane, so it proceeded to jump the guardrail and hurtle down a steep incline.

Almost three years after this horrific accident, Alicia still shuddered every time she recalled it. The fact there were eyewitness accounts as to what had taken place, as well as a police investigation that filled in the details, made the event all the more unsettling.

Alicia tried seeing a therapist to help her deal with debilitating depression, but it seemed better to let time pass and resign herself to a life without the two people she loved. Moving to Clearview was an accomplishment of sorts, as it would have been easier to stay put and continue to wallow in grief. Clearview had been recommended by a fellow teacher who was familiar with it, his reason why was never explained. She liked the place immediately and everyone was friendly. She'd decided to obtain a license to sell insurance, thinking it would be a good choice for a new career. Both her parents had passed away, but they made sure she was "taken care of" in case she could no longer teach and ended up alone, albeit never fathoming the circumstances that would make as much be true.

One thing Alicia liked about her job was she didn't have to drive to it if she didn't want to and usually she didn't. Thanks to what happened she no longer liked to drive unless it was absolutely necessary. Not even inclement weather stopped her from making the trek to and from Brewer Insurance, five days a week. Sometimes it was no small feat to brave the elements, given how much more harsh the weather could be here in Michigan, versus St. Louis.

Alicia's boss, Carl Brewer, claimed she was the most dependable employee he'd ever had. His other full-time employee, Jill Combs, a single mom of three elementary school-age kids, was seemingly always missing work because one of her kids was sick and couldn't go to school. It wasn't long before Mr. Brewer realized how indispensable Alicia was, and that made her feel proud. Not only that it proved she was useful to someone.

Vance Merritt walked into Brewer Insurance one morning, on the pretense of wanting an insurance quote. The truth of the matter was he had seen Alicia having lunch in Maple Park on a number of occasions and he had to get to know her somehow. A woman that striking-looking deserved to be with someone if she wasn't already. Vance happened to be alone in his life, save for his daughter, Angeline. He'd lost his wife, Ruth, in an automobile accident two years ago, when the three of them were living in Spokane, Washington. It was a hit-and-run, and authorities couldn't locate the driver. Vance just wanted his wife back. Given the utter impossibility of that, he was too numb to be bitter. At times it seemed like he might as well have died too. Although Angeline was in the car too, she was miraculously unhurt.

Seeing Alicia Bellcamp for the first time was the best thing that happened to Vance since losing Ruth. Tracking the woman down had made Vance feel alive for the first time since his wife's death. He'd never considered what he was doing "stalking" because he was merely a lonely man in search of a like-minded female. He sensed there was justification in pursuing this woman, despite admittedly lacking any sort of intuition.

Initially Vance wasn't sure if he could go through with his plan. After having confirmed where Alicia worked and what her name was (through her boss), he could hardly keep from just walking in the insurance office and asking her out. He didn't use Brewer Insurance because he used the company next door to his computer repair store, "Computers Unlimited." The former was owned by his brother-in-law Mark (Ruth's younger brother) and his wife, Gretchen. They also owned the building in which Computers Unlimited was located. Vance had a computer repair business in Spokane but wanted to move following Ruth's passing. He was coincidentally invited by Mark to lease the vacant store front for a reasonable sum in perpetuity. The offer was so generous Vance jumped at it and quickly sold his and Ruth's house. In no time at all he had found a suitable place for himself and Angeline and got his business running. He was just busy enough to never be bored but could take an afternoon off here and there and not feel like he was dropping everything.

Poor Angeline. Albeit brave and precocious, she nonetheless had to take on a lot, enduring the sudden death of her mother. Back in Spokane, Vance had taken Angeline to a therapist, thinking she needed to go to one. After the first visit, Angeline pleaded with Vance not to take her there anymore. Also, could they please pretend her mother "went away"? Therefore, they would agree to talk about her as if she were eventually returning home again.

Initially Vance was taken aback by this plea of his daughter's. Then, the more he thought about it, the more it made sense—provided Angeline continued to behave normally otherwise.

Angeline did indeed continue to appear "normal," and her grades improved from Bs and a couple Cs to all As. Vance was too astounded to congratulate her and reasoned maybe it was just as well. Angeline didn't like to draw attention to herself, not even having her efforts acknowledged. She had to have been hurting inside, and a coping mechanism was to apply herself to her studies. She always did appear to have a preference for her mother (over him). Sometimes the similarities between mother and daughter were so striking, he wondered what role he actually played in the creation of such a unique little girl, whose I.Q. was probably off the charts, never mind what her grades were in school.

It was warm and sunny today, versus cold and snowy, as it could be in Clearview by the end of October. As much as Alicia appreciated the unexpectedly pleasant weather, she couldn't help dreading winter. Given Clearview's location, there was inevitably a lot of lake-effect snowfall, which turned her walking commute to and from Brewer Insurance into sheer drudgery.

According to the weather reports, the mild weather was only going to last a few more days before reality set in. By the following week, there were predictions for several inches of snow. In the meantime there was a carnival scheduled for this weekend, the proceeds to benefit the building of a shelter for women recovering from domestic abuse. In smaller towns there didn't seem to be a need for such an establishment, but what did Alicia know? Ever since losing her family she'd been living an isolated existence. Once she was up to it, maybe she could do some volunteer work, perhaps even at the new shelter.

At lunchtime, Alicia took the sack lunch she'd packed and walked the short distance to Maple Park. It was a "habit" she'd begun over the summer, provided the weather was agreeable. With the sun at her back, she sat on a bench and settled down to enjoy herself, food in one hand, paperback novel in the other. She typically read mysteries, Agatha Christie being her favorite author. Thanks to meeting a man by the name of Vance Merritt, however, she was compelled to read some romances. Speaking of him, she hoped he made an appearance, as he said he might do if he was back this way for an appointment. He couldn't guarantee anything, since he ran his business by himself. He'd stopped in the office this morning and after introducing himself, requested a quote for insuring his car, house, and business. She was aware of him intently studying her while she tried to quickly provide some estimates. They had the office to themselves, as Jill wasn't in until 11:30. When Alicia recommended he return later and she'd have the quotes, he said, "To be honest, I was using that as an excuse to introduce myself and spend a little time with you." He mentioned having seen her at the park on many occasions, when he'd be driving by on his way to an "office call." He then "did some research" to find out who she was and exactly where she worked. He added he was "a lonely widower looking for companionship." She could hardly wait to reveal she was a widow, and neither one could believe her/his "good fortune" for having met.

After chatting with Vance for a few minutes, Alicia found out quite a bit about him, including the fact he lived with his eight-year-old daughter, Angeline. Before departing, he gave Alicia his mobile and home phone numbers, as well as his business number, along with his e-mail, all printed on a business card. Meanwhile, she didn't give him anything! The last thing she wanted to do was appear aloof or disinterested in him, but that was undoubtedly how she ended up portraying herself. The logical solution was to simply contact Vance in the near future, but she didn't see things that way. All she cared about was not looking lonely or needy (although she would have readily admitted to being both).

Alicia endlessly beat herself up regarding not giving Vance her number (she only had a land line) to the point she could hardly concentrate the rest of the work day. Jill was on the phone most of the time, but it didn't sound business-related, given how much she giggled. Five o'clock couldn't come fast enough. Fortunately Jill preferred making up her hours by staying later, so it worked out well for Alicia. Otherwise she'd probably stay longer each day, if only because she had nothing else to do anyway.

After leaving Brewer Insurance, Alicia went to her favorite grocery store of the two in Clearview, "Fresh-4-U." She liked it because it had a gourmet section where you could sit down and enjoy your carry-out order. It was more relaxing sitting there than in a fast food restaurant, the only other place she'd dine alone.

Alicia wanted to pick up a couple items and wasn't up to pushing a cart around the store, so a hand basket would do. Besides, since she'd walked to work, she'd be carrying her purchases home.

In no time at all, Alicia's hand basket was brimming with too many items for the express check stand. Usually she didn't have to wait long at this store, no matter what register she used, but on this particular day there seemed to be a hang-up of some sort at every one. Feeling overwhelmed by as much, she proceeded to set her basket down between check stands four and five. Then she heard Vance say from behind her, "Alicia! Great to see you here!" She turned around and there stood Vance with a half-full cart of groceries as well as whom she presumed to be his daughter, Angeline. When talking about her earlier in the day, he'd said it all when declaring, "Angeline's my life." Alicia had the distinct pleasure of being introduced to the little girl, and Alicia was described to her as "the nice lady I met at Brewer Insurance."

Alicia considered it appropriate to shake hands with Angeline, although the girl appeared a bit taken aback by the gesture. Nonetheless she did manage to give Alicia a firm handshake, which was impressive, given how otherwise shy she appeared to be. Seeing this girl might have made Alicia pine for her daughter, but it was impossible to make a connection. Maybe she was too caught up in her feelings for Vance. It was almost as if there was an electrical charge between them that went deeper than what she'd felt for Troy. She was ashamed of as much and felt as if she were betraying her husband.

After shaking hands with Alicia, Angeline was quick to retreat to her father's side, which he didn't appear to notice. Possibly the girl was afraid of Alicia. Other than that, Alicia didn't know what to make of her, other than she seemed kind of weird.

Vance asked, "Are you picking up a few things?"

"I can never buy only a couple items, even if I know I have to walk home with all of it," Alicia replied.

"Why don't you skip making dinner tonight and join us?" he asked and then added, "I make a super lasagna, just ask Angeline."

Alicia saw Angeline nod after her father made his remark, so Alicia found herself nodding too, unintentionally accepting the invitation. She wanted to say, "Thanks. Some other time," but Angeline said, "We always have lots of leftovers," helping confirm the invite.

Vance jumped in, adding, "We sure do. Come on over, Alicia. You'll save us from having to eat lasagna three nights in a row. Six-thirty, seven? What'll work best for you?"

"Six-thirty," she answered. Earlier was better because Alicia could hardly wait to be going somewhere for dinner.

Meanwhile, check stands four and five were finally moving again, so Alicia went to the left (number four) with her hand basket, and Vance pushed his cart to number five. Angeline immediately set to work, unloading everything onto the conveyor belt.

The cashier at check stand four told Alicia to place the hand basket on the conveyor belt and leave all the items in it. Therefore, Alicia was at her leisure to continue chatting with Vance, who told her, "I'll write down the directions to our house on the grocery receipt, if you don't mind waiting a minute. It's close to downtown, but it's kind of hard to find."

"My friends get lost," Angeline declared.

"Don't you live in a cul-de-sac?" Alicia asked, trying to recall exactly what Vance had mentioned about where he and Angeline lived. As the crow flew, their house wasn't far from Alicia's, but she planned on driving there.

Vance not only wrote the directions on the back of his grocery receipt but gave Alicia his home phone number again. It wasn't until he left with his daughter did it occur to Alicia to ask him for a ride home. Undoubtedly he would have been happy to oblige.

Alicia had the office to herself the following morning, thanks to an excused absence from Jill. Their boss, Carl Brewer, wasn't around much and put a lot of trust in Alicia and Jill to keeping his business running smoothly. Alicia cherished the responsibility.

Things were slow, so Alicia had plenty of time to review the events of last evening. Vance's lasagna was absolutely delicious and not only because Alicia had a favorable opinion of the cook. He confessed to having learned several recipes from his mother and aunt, as he'd taken an interest in cooking, in his early teens. Since he was also a computer nerd, the latter had decided his livelihood.

Angeline didn't say a word at the dinner table, other than "please" and "thank you" when the lasagna and a bowl of salad greens were passed around. It was entirely unmistakable: Angeline did not want Alicia in her (Angeline's) and her father's beautiful Victorian-style house EVER. Admittedly it was a loaded assumption that was possibly just that and nothing more. It was easy to draw the wrong conclusion about an acquaintance when you spent too much time alone. Having read several self-help books following the deaths of Troy and Claudia, Alicia was made aware of what isolating herself could do to her psyche.

After dinner, Vance and Alicia drank decaffeinated coffee, and Angeline went upstairs to take a bath and finish her homework. Vance had already shown Alicia the house and what projects he was undertaking to continue restoring it, so Angeline didn't have to worry about being interrupted. At first it didn't appear there was anything particularly atypical about Angeline's bedroom – posters of animals were all over the sky blue walls, as well as some of male and female pop stars. However, there was an absence of any toys, dolls, or stuffed animals, all of which seemed appropriate for a girl her age. Instead she had a large, white wicker bookcase filled with books. Alicia commented about Angeline's impressive library, and Vance revealed his daughter got the reading bug from her mother, Ruth. Also, Angeline had a thing about actual, physical books and wasn't into technology as much as her friends already were.

Truthfully, Alicia was ambivalent about the evening she spent with Vance and Angeline. Since the latter was silent for the most part, maybe that really did "say it all" about the girl. Vance hinted he hadn't dated anyone since he lost Ruth. Therefore, Alicia had "broken the ice" by agreeing to have dinner with him and Angeline.

The phone rang and it was Vance. Alicia's whole body felt like it fluttered upon hearing him greet her. He proceeded to thank her for accepting his dinner invitation and hoped she'd enjoyed herself. She told him she did and thanked him for having invited her. She also complimented him on his cooking skills, which she had done the evening before, as well. Vance thanked her and said she was welcome for dinner, anytime. In turn, Alicia thanked him for the open invitation, hoping her enthusiasm showed her appreciation. Although the two remained acquaintances, there was no denying she felt something very real for him. Having Vance call her the morning following their "date" was encouraging.

Not only that, Vance said, "Alicia, I'd like to get together with you again, soon. I want to get to know you."

"I'd like to get to know you, too," Alicia said.

Bolstered by Alicia's declaration, Vance went on to tell her, "I know Angeline likes you, which is no small feat. By the way, I have to leave town early Wednesday morning and I'll be back Friday. I'll call you as soon as I get home."

"What about Angeline?"

"Misses Morrison will be staying with her in our house. She lives in that big, two-story with the wraparound porch, on the corner of Beech and Lancaster. She ran that as a boarding house for years, after her husband Joe passed. They raised seven kids there."

Already Alicia couldn't wait until Vance contacted her again. She was falling for him by the minute and enjoying every second of it.

Saturday morning there had yet to be a call from Vance, and Alicia had even given him her home phone number when they last spoke. Although she could have called him, she was determined to be patient. In the meantime, she called "The Hair Repair" and made an appointment for a haircut with Lindy, her regular stylist. The only problem was Lindy couldn't take Alicia for a whole week, so more waiting was in order.

The call finished, the phone rang again, and this time it was Vance. Alicia was so relieved to hear from him, she felt light-headed. After exchanging pleasantries, he said, "I got back later than I'd expected yesterday, so I thought it was better to wait until this morning to call you."

Amy Kristoff

Alicia wanted to chat with Vance for a minute or two, but he couldn't seem to wait to say, "Angeline wants to talk to you. O.K. if I put her on?"

The next thing Alicia knew, she was saying good morning to shy little Angeline, who didn't sound so shy today. In fact, she had a favor to ask of Alicia: "Could you please take me to the carnival today?"

"What time?" she asked, shocked by the suddenness of the request.

"Right now."

The back of Alicia's neck felt prickly. Evidently she did not imagine earlier, this kid was a spoiled brat. Alicia wanted nothing more than to do what the little girl wished, but it didn't seem prudent. If her father wanted to spoil her, that was his business. At the same time, it was hard to say no to a brat, especially when wanting to please the brat's father. Therefore, Alicia ended up saying, "I can be ready in half an hour and I'll be right over."

"I'll see you then," Angeline said and started to hang up when Vance was heard in the background, telling her to wait a second.

"I hope this is all right with you, Alicia," Vance said. "Angeline is very eager to get together with you."

"Yes, it's great," Alicia told him, uncertain as to what to say. Truthfully she didn't agree with Vance's take on the matter, nor was she looking forward to spending time alone with his daughter, at least not yet.

Vance and Angeline were standing next to one another on the bottom step of the porch when Alicia pulled up in her newer, dark blue Chevrolet Impala. Alicia waved at the same time Vance did. Although Angeline didn't wave, she was smiling, looking the happiest Alicia had ever seen her. Then Angeline turned to her father and said something.

"Good morning!" Vance said when Alicia stepped out of her car. "It's the perfect day for an outing, isn't it?"

Alicia agreed and added, "I don't know how the carnival

coordinators could have known the weather would be so mild this late in the year, so I guess they took their chances."

"They sure did and they totally lucked out," Vance said and then asked Angeline, "Are you ready, sweetheart?"

After Angeline hugged her father, she hurried over to Alicia, who was standing about halfway between her car and the porch. Angeline looked up at her and said, "Thank you for coming."

Alicia was so undone by this one comment from Angeline, she concluded the poor girl wasn't a brat after all and simply needed understanding. She'd lost her mother at a young age, and it was only natural for her father to pander to her, making her appear spoiled.

Alicia helped Angeline get in the passenger side of the car and made sure the seat belt was fastened. As Alicia was getting in the driver's side she couldn't help thinking about how no one had been in a car with her for three years, let alone a young girl. It was time to welcome changes in her life and learn how to enjoy herself again.

"You two have fun," Vance called. Angeline waved in response.

Fortunately the site of the carnival – the parking lot of St. Anthony School – wasn't far because uneasy feelings returned as soon as Vance's and Angeline's house was out of sight. Trying to make conversation, Alicia asked Angeline, "How's school?" to which she replied, "Fine. My teacher, Miss Holly, says I could be a doctor if I wanted because I'm so smart. I think I'd rather be a veterinarian because I like animals a lot."

"That's good, knowing what you want to be at your age."

"I have a friend, Dawn, who wants to be a nurse 'cause her mom is one. She doesn't have a father like I don't have a mother, but that's only 'cause mine went away. Her dad cheated on her mom and dumped her."

Alicia wasn't sure how to respond to that remark, so she said, "That's too bad. I don't know if your father told you, but

Amy Kristoff

I lost my husband and daughter in a traffic accident three years ago. My daughter was the same age as you and her name was Claudia."

Angeline just nodded, so Alicia didn't know if Vance had told her this or not. Alicia only brought as much up so the girl wouldn't feel so alone. Maybe she should have waited to mention anything about her daughter.

Suddenly Angeline wanted to know, "Did Claudia look like me?"

Alicia glanced at her before replying, "I suppose somewhat." There was in fact a faint semblance: the petite frame; the narrow face; the upturned nose; and the widely-set, sparkling blue eyes. However, Angeline had fine, wavy, shoulder-length blond hair, while Claudia's was medium-brown and shorter, as well as much thicker.

Alicia's reply appeared to satisfy Angeline, and she didn't ask if Alicia happened to have a photo of Claudia in her wallet. She did, and it was one of Claudia standing next to her father at the entrance of Disneyworld in Orlando, Florida. The three of them spent five days there after Christmas Day, the year before Claudia turned eight, which would be the last year of her life.

Alicia shivered at the thought and bit her lip to keep from crying, having reminded herself she had company here in the car. If she "lost it," Vance would hear all about it, and that would eliminate any hope for Alicia and him to establish a relationship, which she wanted more than anything.

Arriving at St. Anthony School, Alicia had to park in the outer reaches because it was so busy. The perfect weather had evidently induced more people than ever to attend the carnival.

Admission was two dollars for adults, and children under twelve were admitted for free. Angeline zeroed in on the grizzled-looking man at the temporary entrance gate and then asked Alicia, "Think that man'll let me in without having to pay?"

"Sure he will," Alicia told her.

"Aw, I was hoping I looked older."

Alicia smiled and said, "Trust me, when you get to be my age, you'll want to look as young as possible."

They had to stand in line for a minute, so Angeline remarked, "My dad tells me I look like my mom."

Alicia looked at Angeline and declared, "There's definitely some similarities between you and your father, but maybe you do look more like your mother." If there was a photograph of Ruth Merritt in Vance's and Angeline's house, Alicia didn't see it. Maybe Vance tucked any pictures of her away for safekeeping.

Finally they reached the admission gate, and after Alicia gave the man the exact change and received two tickets, Angeline couldn't help but ask, "How did that guy really know for sure I'm under twelve?"

"He probably assumed I'm your mother and I would never sneak you in here for free. It wouldn't be so bad to pay an extra two dollars, since the money's going to a good cause."

The two walked no more than twenty feet when a vendor called, "Hey Mom and girlie, three balls for a quarter. Everybody's a winner, even if you miss the bull's eye."

"Maybe on the way out," Alicia told the creep, who leered at her. This was going to become humiliating yet. Or it already was but she was too lacking in self-esteem to notice. She took Angeline's hand and led her away. Angeline was initially reluctant, until seeing some ponies tied to a contraption that looked like a circular clothesline. The few occasions Alicia had taken Claudia to a carnival or county fair, a pony ride had consisted of an actual ride on a pony in a designated area, usually on sand or grass. These ponies were forced to walk around and around on the blacktop. There couldn't have been a worse fate for the poor creatures. Worse still, they were all depressed-looking, hairy and fat. At the moment there wasn't anyone interested in riding them, so it was tempting to consider it an option. Then it occurred to

Amy Kristoff

Alicia, letting Angeline ride a pony might get the girl started on liking horses and even becoming obsessed with them. Vance would have every right to blame Alicia for as much.

"How about we ride the Ferris wheel?" Alicia asked and they did. After that they rode the Scrambler and the Tilt-a-Whirl. Then it was time for lunch, as Angeline let it be known she was hungry. Alicia asked her if she would first like to ride the merry-go-round, since no one was interested it, not unlike the pony rides. (Alicia figured Angeline wouldn't become horse crazy from riding the inanimate version.) Everyone appeared to prefer either the "thrill rides" or the "three for a quarter games." Hopefully the guy who called to her at the carnival entrance would be as busy as all his comrades when Angeline and she made their exit.

Angeline took one look at the merry-go-round and declared she didn't want to ride it. Perhaps if some of the horses went up and down, the ride would have had more allure.

There was quite a line at the concession stand, but it seemed to be moving rather quickly. In the meantime they could read the extensive menu, displayed on a white plastic sign above and behind the counter. Alicia asked Angeline if she could see it all right, and she said she could. Alicia then wanted to know if Angeline wanted to order for herself, or did she want Alicia to do so?

"I'll say what I want," Angeline declared and soon afterward did so: "I'd like a large root beer, cotton candy, a 'king-sized' Hershey bar, a bag of caramel corn, and an ice cream sandwich."

Meanwhile, Alicia looked through her wallet to make sure she had enough money to pay for everything. Then she ordered a hot dog with ketchup and a small lemonade. It never occurred to her what could happen to Angeline if she even attempted to eat all the items she'd just ordered. All Alicia could think about was pleasing Vance's daughter.

Angeline got through the ice cream sandwich, half the

caramel corn, some of the cotton candy, a few sips of the root beer and a couple bites of the Hershey bar before grinding to a halt and announcing she wasn't feeling well. Simultaneously she began looking pale and uncomfortable. As an afterthought she added, "I think I ate too much of the wrong things" and clutched her stomach.

"We'd better get you home," Alicia said, getting up, leaving a couple bites of her hot dog and most of her lemonade.

Angeline followed Alicia to the car, carrying the rest of the caramel corn, despite her condition. Alicia was entirely oblivious because she was consumed by what Vance was going to think. After all, there was no doubt Alicia was to blame for this.

Driving back to Vance's and Angeline's, trying to hurry yet not speed, Alicia remarked, "Your father is going to be surprised to see us so soon," and Angeline nodded as she continued to hold her stomach, the remainder of the bag of caramel corn beside her.

Just as Alicia was turning into the driveway, Angeline suddenly leaned forward and proceeded to throw up all over herself, the floor, the dashboard, the seat, and the caramel corn bag.

Vance was obviously looking out for them, as he emerged from the house almost instantaneously, which was a relief. However, Alicia dreaded having him see what just happened. When he did, he said, "I'll get some towels" and went back inside. Meanwhile, Alicia got out of the car and went to the passenger side to extricate Angeline from the mess. The girl appeared entirely defeated but no longer sick. She probably didn't appreciate having her father worried about the interior of Alicia's car before anything else.

"Really, you don't have to do this," Alicia said as she was being driven home by Vance. After cleaning her car the best he could, he insisted she leave it with him so he could have a friend detail it. The guy worked for someone during the week but did "freelance detailing" on the weekend.

"It's the least I can do," Vance told her. He was embarrassed. Angeline was technically the one at fault, having confessed to gorging herself on junk food. He never should have let her call Alicia and ask her to take her to the carnival. Actually he made the call and let Angeline make the much-desired request. What was it with her? She was usually standoffish with people she didn't know, occasionally even with him.

Vance was absolutely wild for Alicia, so that alone affected his judgement. In other words, he shouldn't have let his daughter take advantage of Alicia's kindness the way he did. He definitely owed it to Alicia, to make sure her car was expertly cleaned, and his vehicle-detailing friend, Jeff Baker, would have it looking like new by Sunday afternoon if not before. Alicia said she didn't need her car any sooner because she liked to walk most places anyway.

The two were nearing Alicia's house by this time and Vance said, "Angeline's not good at expressing herself, but I do know she sincerely regrets what happened. She was too humiliated to say much."

"I understand," Alicia said. She didn't want Vance to go on and on about his cherished daughter because she did not share his sentiments about the girl. Angeline was probably sorry, but that didn't change what she did. Not only that, Vance couldn't have been too surprised by what happened. The bottom line was Alicia didn't think Angeline was shy at all and was in fact precocious and destined to be quite promiscuous if her father didn't open his eyes. Angeline needed a mother-figure, but Alicia wasn't about to tell Vance any of this for one reason: she was afraid of Angeline.

Vance dropped Alicia off at her house and told her, "I really appreciate you taking Angeline to the carnival today. I know she had a great time, despite her indiscretion. She thinks a lot of you."

Alicia couldn't believe Vance's assessment of his daughter! She vowed to trust her instincts before anything else.

The phone rang Sunday morning, and Alicia wasn't even close to feeling awake. Vance was the caller, first apologizing if he'd awakened her. Usually she didn't sleep past seven-thirty on Sundays, but the events of the day before had exhausted her, so it was probably pretty late. Rather than ask Vance what time it was (and feel like an even bigger dope) she checked her digital alarm clock: it was nine-thirty!

Vance wanted to know if it was all right to return her car, and Alicia could drive him home.

"Wow, that was fast," Alicia remarked.

"Jeff made you his priority. I'd told him you had to walk everywhere otherwise."

"I walk a lot instead of driving, but it's still nice knowing I'll have my car back."

"Have you eaten breakfast yet?"

"No."

"How about when I bring your car over, we go out? My treat." Chuckling, Vance added, "The only problem with that scenario is we'll be in your car."

Alicia laughed. Then she was asked what time would it be O.K. to pick her up? Vance was undoubtedly ready but she sure as heck wasn't. As much as she wanted to see Vance again, she needed some time to look presentable. Sensing he was anxious to get moving for the day, she told him she'd be ready in forty-five minutes.

Before hanging up, Alicia asked Vance, "Is Angeline accompanying us?" hoping her true feelings about the girl weren't evident.

"Mrs. Morrison took Angeline with her to church," Vance replied, sounding like it was common knowledge.

"The Kitchen" was Vance's favorite place for breakfast, and patrons seated themselves. He had a favorite booth in the far right corner, by the window. There he could read the paper and simultaneously keep an eye on the Route 36 traffic. It was more interesting than people-watching.

Vance led Alicia to "his" booth, where there were already two place settings. Usually there weren't any, and the waitress would give him one when she appeared with a coffee cup and a pot of coffee. The menus remained on the table, tucked behind the salt and pepper shaker holder. As it was, Vance didn't need to bother reading the menu because he had it memorized. Whenever he brought Angeline, she seemed miserable, so maybe he'd been selfish for dragging her along. It was refreshing to come here with someone who enjoyed a restaurant like this as much as he did.

As Alicia perused the menu, Vance recommended the pancakes with Canadian bacon. That sounded like too much to eat, so she decided on a whole wheat English muffin and an order of bacon. It would be the most she ever ate in the morning.

After they'd ordered, Vance said, "There's something I would like to tell you."

Immediately Alicia assumed the worst, as in Vance was about to confess something sordid about his personal life. She probably appeared apprehensive because she was!

Finally, he said, "Angeline was with her mother when the car accident occurred, but she has no recollection of any events prior to it nor does she remember the accident itself. And she prefers to pretend her mother went away, versus died. I've accepted that notion myself, at this point, but in the early going it was tough on me. I had a lot of pictures of Ruth as well as personal items to put away! What bothers me to this day is I'm almost certain she distracted her mother for a second, but I don't know for sure. What's inexplicable is Ruth wasn't wearing her seat belt yet she always did. Angeline was wearing hers though, thankfully, and she survived without a scratch."

Alicia couldn't help but notice Vance's hand movements when he was talking, and they seemed to tell more than what he was actually saying. In other words he appeared to be more agonized by what had happened to his wife than he let on, if only because it was possible their daughter had something to do with it, perhaps even intentionally.

Breakfast arrived, coffee cups were refilled, and Vance and Alicia ate, not conversing much. As the meal wound down, Vance said, "I'd like to invite you to lunch tomorrow. Let's take advantage of the last of this spectacular weather and go to the lakefront. I have a spot in mind, and we'll hopefully have it to ourselves."

"I have to work," Alicia responded.

Rather than take issue with her reluctance, Vance told her, "Come on, Alicia. You told me how you never missed a day at Brewer's. That deserves a reward."

How Alicia saw it was, she had a perfect attendance record, so why mess it up? She shook her head in reply to Vance's urging.

Refusing to give up, Vance said, "Everybody needs a little time off. I bet your boss puts in a fraction of the hours you and Jill do."

Alicia admitted, "He isn't around much, but he's probably off doing something business-related."

"Brewer must think he struck gold with you for an employee," Vance remarked. "Your dedication is admirable."

"Thank you."

"I intend to cancel some plans for tomorrow late morning and part of the afternoon, provided I can get you to play hooky with me."

Because Alicia didn't want to disappoint Vance was the biggest reason why she agreed to call in sick tomorrow morning. She dreaded doing so, as it would mark her as a liar for the rest of her life.

Alicia proceeded to do as she'd promised, calling Mr. Brewer's house at eight o'clock the next morning to tell him she couldn't make it to work. There was at least one screaming child in the background, which didn't help the situation.

He made no secret of not being pleased about the news, which almost compelled her to change her mind. Then Mr. Brewer said, "Clearly the flu bug's hit your house too. My wife and I are dealing with a couple cases of it here, which probably sounds pretty obvious from your end. Rest up and I'll see you tomorrow."

There. Alicia had her day off, her boss didn't suspect a thing, and she was going to spend part of the day with a man she barely knew but was totally crazy about. She didn't want for anything more – other than to be able to decide what to wear for the occasion.

Vance's car horn could be heard about 10:55, a little later than when he said he'd pick her up. Nonetheless she was still styling her hair. Lindy had to reschedule Alicia's appointment, so there would be several more days' wait.

Alicia grabbed a jacket before heading out the door, although it was possible she wouldn't need it. The weather was positively fabulous, so the T-shirt and jeans she had on, were enough. Then again, they were having lunch at the lakefront.

"Sorry I'm a little late," Vance said when he got out of his white Chevy Sonic to help Alicia get in the passenger side. "By the way, you look great."

"Thank you." This was definitely the best Alicia had felt in she didn't know how long.

It took about fifty minutes to reach their destination, as Vance drove on the slower, more scenic Route 14, rather than Thirty-six. He remarked, "Hey, look. No mobile phone, just us. That's a new one for me. Lately it's been one thing or another, so it's a relief to just drop everything and leave for a few hours."

Alicia was more and more glad she took the day off. She was looking forward to enjoying the picnic lunch Vance had prepared. He'd been a little late picking her up because he was still gathering items for the picnic basket.

Once the two of them arrived at the parking area overlooking the lakefront (they had the whole place to themselves), Vance suggested they go for a walk before lunch, to help work up their appetites. Alicia didn't bother mentioning how hungry she already was, having skipped breakfast.

They walked along the lakefront for half an hour, passing a number of beach houses, many of them quite impressive-looking. Vance then declared it was time to return to the car, as the wind had started to pick up.

Vance pulled a large wicker basket out of the back of his car, and Alicia remarked, "That looks heavy. I hope there's more than just food in there."

"I also have china and silverware in here," he replied. "Maybe we could sit close by." There happened to be an open, level spot of beach between the end of the gravel parking lot and the dune grass.

After Vance had laid out a brown wool blanket, Alicia plopped down on it, eagerly waiting to be served. He made two place settings, including brown linen napkins. Just as she was about to unfold her napkin, a small, maroon velvet jewelry box tumbled out. She opened it to find a stunning, yellow-gold diamond ring that had to have cost Vance a small fortune.

"It's beautiful. Thank you," Alicia said, not wanting to appear to be assuming he was about to propose marriage. Even if she fantasized about as much, emotionally she was completely unprepared.

Looking pleased with himself, Vance said, "I don't mean to put any pressure on you, but I'd liked for us to be exclusive so we can really get to know one another. So the ring is first and foremost a 'friendship ring,' but I hope it can also eventually be an engagement ring. Either way, it's yours to keep."

There was no doubt Alicia saw tears in Vance's eyes. Before she removed the ring from the box, he scooted next to her and gave her a kiss. "I love you," he told her afterward, going completely against his vow to wait longer before declaring as much. He was reassured, however, by having Alicia tell him she loved him, too.

The only problem was the ring didn't fit. Vance told Alicia he'd purchased it at the only jewelry store in Clearview, "Fitzpatrick's," and it could be sized at no extra cost. They could stop in there on the way home.

Alicia didn't want it to be a big deal, so she said, "I can take care of it tomorrow."

"No, Alicia. Please. It won't be out of our way at all."

After packing up, Vance and Alicia headed to the jewelry store, taking the main route into town, Thirty-six, which got them stuck in a huge traffic jam. That only happened if there was an accident. He looked at Alicia and asked her, "Are you thinking what I'm thinking?" and she nodded. Her complexion was deathly pale, as her mind immediately went back to the day she lost the two most important people in her life.

Finally near the scene of the accident itself, there was a tow truck, an ambulance, and three Clearview police cars. However, it appeared the "accident" was little more than an older, white panel truck with a dented front fender, the driver standing beside it looking dazed. Meanwhile the first responders were standing off to the side, looking confused, too.

By the time Vance and Alicia reached the jewelry store, even he was anxious. He attributed the feeling to not having his cell phone. Suddenly there was nothing valiant about being unavailable when you had a young daughter to raise on your own. So much for being cavalier about his brief unavailability.

Usually Fitzpatrick's wasn't busy, so the fact only one employee manned the store at a time, wasn't an issue. On this particular day, however, there were three customers ahead of Vance and Alicia, and Jim, the owner, was here alone (aside from a jeweler in the back). Again Alicia tried to persuade Vance to wait until another time, but he was adamant they stay.

When it was their turn, Jim took one look at Alicia and

exclaimed, "I know you! You're the one I see walking everywhere."

"I'm Alicia Bellcamp. I work at Brewer Insurance and walk to work every day."

"Nice to meet you. How come I didn't see you today?"

Smiling, Alicia replied, "I took the day off, after some hesitation, I must add." Then she looked at Vance, who smiled too. She assumed this guy didn't know her boss, at least not very well. At the moment she didn't care because she felt like she was in exactly the place in life she needed to be.

The ring was sized in no time and would be ready in two days, possibly sooner, no charge (as promised at the time of purchase). Alicia gave Jim her phone number and she looked forward to picking it up. It didn't matter if she and Vance married anytime soon; all she cared about at this point was his vote of approval.

Driving Alicia home, Vance said, "See? That wasn't so bad. If you'd waited until tomorrow to take the ring in, it'd be an extra day you'd have to wait to wear it."

"You're right. Thanks again, for the ring and the wonderful day."

"You're welcome," Vance said, taking Alicia's hand in his.

At Alicia's, Vance got out of the car and escorted her to the front door. After kissing her good-bye, he said he'd call her later. He then added, would she in fact care to join him and Angeline for dinner?

After Alicia told Vance she was fine staying home for the evening, Vance said, "Just remember, you're always welcome at our house. I might have already told you that, but I honestly can't emphasize it enough."

"Thank you," Alicia said, hoping Vance didn't become insistent about his "open invitation." She wanted some time to think about everything.

The luxury of "time to reflect" existed for about twenty minutes and the phone rang. The second Alicia heard Vance's voice she knew something was wrong and it most likely involved Angeline. Indeed, Vance proceeded to tell her, "I sure messed up this afternoon. I'd proudly told you how no one could get ahold of me when we were on our little excursion, and Angeline became ill at school and needed to be sent home, but of course that was impossible."

"Is it something serious?" Alicia asked and Vance replied, "I'm not sure. I'm leaving right now to pick her up. I feel like a careless idiot at the moment."

"Does this have to do with the food she ate Saturday?" Alicia asked, mostly thinking aloud.

"No, I don't think so," Vance replied. "She's been fine since that incident and was fine this morning. Before she left for the bus stop, I told her I was spending part of the day with you."

"You did?"

"Yes," Vance said, missing the obvious, as in Angeline "became ill" to get attention.

It was becoming increasingly plain, Angeline was none too keen to "share" her father, especially after having him to herself.

Alicia was going to Vance's (and Angeline's) for dinner after work this evening. Truthfully she didn't want to go. Angeline gave her the creeps, and the feeling was unshakable. Because Alicia would have to love them both, it was necessary for her to stop seeing Vance. The bottom line was she couldn't imagine ever loving Angeline.

Tonight, when Angeline hopefully left them alone for a few minutes, Alicia intended to tell Vance it was over. She also would return the ring, as soon as she picked it up at the jewelry store the following afternoon.

As it turned out, nothing had been the matter with Angeline when she became sick at school the day before. Vance had called Alicia again when he got home with his daughter. He actually sounded mad at her for having made him look like a negligent father. Alicia didn't feel a whole lot of sympathy for him because he did nothing to stop his only child from ruling his world.

In the meantime, the work day at Brewer Insurance was interminable. All Alicia could think about was what she should tell Vance. She didn't want to hurt him, but she had to look out for herself. Unfortunately, there was no way to portray Angeline favorably, in regard to her attitude toward Alicia. Meanwhile, Vance had himself convinced otherwise. That proved the best thing Alicia could do was cut ties with them both. Then she got an idea: show up with a bottle of wine, even something pricey. Vance claimed he wasn't much for drinking but did imbibe from time to time. Hopefully it would help keep the mood of the evening, relaxed.

On the way to Vance's and Angeline's, Alicia stopped at her favorite supermarket and picked up some wine, already chilled.

"What a fantastic idea!" Vance said when he greeted Alicia at the door with her bottle of wine. Taking it from her, he leaned over and kissed her. Then he put his arm around her, guiding her inside. She hardly expected such an "intimate" reception, which only made her feel worse about what she intended to tell him later.

Heading to the kitchen with Alicia on his arm, Vance told her, "Angeline's chopping boiled egg for the salad."

Alicia couldn't help asking, "Is she inspired to be Dad's little helper?"

"Yes, she is," he replied, smiling. "I think she considers this quite an event. I know I keep saying it, but she really likes you and wants to redeem herself, especially after what happened over the past weekend."

Alicia nodded in acknowledgement of what Vance told her, but as soon as she fell in step behind him, she couldn't help rolling her eyes.

In the terra-cotta-colored tile kitchen, which easily fulfilled a devoted cook's wish list, Angeline was standing to the left of the sink, still working on putting the salad together.

Alicia greeted her by saying, "Hi, Angeline. How are you?"

"I'm fine, thank you," she replied, briefly turning to make eye contact.

Alicia wanted to ask Angeline if she was feeling better than when she had to leave school early, but she didn't have it in her. Besides, Vance appeared to be the one most hurt by what her daughter did.

Vance proceeded to tend to what was on the stove and check what was in the oven. Afterward he announced dinner would be ready in a couple minutes. Angeline finished preparing the salad and happened to notice the bottle of wine sitting on the counter. Pointing at it, she asked her father, "Can I have some of that too?"

"I guess you could honey, why not."

Alicia was positively floored. Maybe she was overreacting, but Angeline appeared to be growing up awfully fast as it was. By the time she was a teenager, nothing would be new to her. Perhaps that was Vance's plan. Whatever the case, Alicia vowed not to say a word.

Before there was any mention of dessert, following an extremely delicious beef stroganoff dinner, Angeline excused herself to work on her report for Science class.

"I thought you finished it," Vance called to her as she ascended the long, wide wooden staircase.

"I have to change a couple things," she replied while rapidly departing, making the last two words barely audible.

If that was the extent of the farewell Alicia received from Angeline, it was fine with her. However, Vance studied where his daughter went long after she'd disappeared, clearly annoyed. Alicia was thrilled. He had to see his daughter for who she was, if he ever again wanted a serious relationship with a woman.

Vance suggested they take their wine glasses outside and sit on the front porch swing. Since the weather was still unbelievably mild, it was an excellent idea. He offered her a refill for her wine, but she didn't need one. This was perfect because Alicia had yet to mention her decision about their relationship, so the more physically distant they could be from Angeline, the better.

Once the two were settled on the swing, Vance put his free arm around her (the one not holding the wine glass). They sat together for a minute before he said, "Not to invite myself over, but if you would like to get together at your house, I'd gladly give Mrs. Morrison a call. She never minds watching Angeline."

That did it. Alicia had no choice but to state her case: "There's something I really need to tell you."

"Uh-oh. Your turn to spill the beans today?" Vance quipped, although there was no humor in his tone of voice.

"It's about us. And the ring. I love it and appreciate the gesture, but I think you should have it back."

"Is it still at the jeweler's?"

"Yes," Alicia replied, "and after I pick it up tomorrow, I want to bring it to you."

"And what am I expected to infer from this?" Vance wanted to know, clearly thunderstruck. "I mean, giving you the ring was supposed to help make you feel comfortable, not compel you to bolt."

"I think we should take a step back and just be friends."

"We have! We are!" Vance retorted, clearly exasperated. He felt like he was going to lose this elusive woman, despite how subtle he tried to be. There was no doubt he loved her or he would have already given up. Attempting to salvage his dignity, he said, "Obviously I was mistaken about what we had together so far. Therefore, I would in fact like the ring back."

Alicia could hear and feel Vance's tenseness as he was talking, even though he no longer had his arm around her. She'd feared things would get ugly, which was why she'd thought long and hard before bringing up this delicate subject.

Amy Kristoff

Taking a final emotional swing at her, Vance said, "Alicia, I want you to know I'm feeling very naïve and stupid at the moment."

It was impossible for Alicia to keep from crying, as there was so much she wanted to say, but doing so would include revealing her reservations about Angeline.

Alicia's crying made Vance realize something serious was going on, and her aloofness was nothing personal. Before she knew it, he leaned over and locked his lips on hers. All she could manage to do was kiss him back, encouraged by his audacity and surprised by her own.

After seemingly no time at all, the kissing ended and Vance turned his head, saying, "Angeline, honey, I thought you were finishing your report."

Alicia didn't want to look at Angeline but did so, and the girl's scowl was so deep her eyes appeared to be two thick, dark lines, on the verge of joining with her eyebrows. Or maybe the wine was making her vision fuzzy. Either way, Alicia was positive beyond a doubt Angeline hated her and always would.

Staring at Alicia, Angeline finally said, "I finished it just now, and I came downstairs to tell you I'm going to bed."

"And I need to be going," Alicia announced, standing. She felt more awkward than ever, thanks to the surprise visit from Angeline, who had already disappeared.

Vance said, "I'm sorry Angeline left before she could say good-bye, so I'll say it on her behalf."

"That's O.K. I don't think she likes me."

Vance burst into laughter in response to Alicia's remark, which she chalked up to relief on his part. In other words, he was able to realize a lot of what was going on in Alicia's head. All Vance considered necessary to do for reassurance was to passionately kiss Alicia, this time in the foyer. It never occurred to either one of them Angeline might be watching.

The morning following Alicia's "final dinner" with Vance

and Angeline, she had a brainstorm: it was time for a career change and a move to a warmer climate. Why suffer through the impossibly long, harsh Michigan winters?

That question remained in Alicia's head as she walked to work. It was windy and the sky was gray. Although the temperature was still rather moderate, it was supposed to drop to freezing by nightfall. In the meantime, there was a good chance of rain by afternoon, and it would be changing to snow. Although the forecast for several inches had been cancelled, it still sounded miserable. Besides, there was no denying the fact winter was coming.

Unfortunately Alicia had left the house without dressing properly for inclement weather. She was wearing a thinly-insulated, nylon jacket over a cotton turtleneck. Even if she made it to work without getting wet, she could plan on an extremely uncomfortable walk home. She wondered if she was doomed to always feeling distracted, which even affected her ability to dress properly.

A big, fat, cold raindrop fell. Then another. And another. Wasn't the rain supposed to wait awhile?

Then an older, silver Mercury Marquis, going the same direction as herself, pulled up to the curb, stopping on the wrong side of the street. It was obvious the driver wanted to speak with Alicia, so she approached the opened driver's side window, and a white-haired woman asked, "Are you on your way to town, young lady? I'll be more than happy to give you a ride."

"Thanks for the offer," Alicia said, "but I'd better keep walking. "I might get the seat wet."

"Nonsense, that's no excuse," the woman replied. "Hop in and get warm. I'll gladly take you wherever you need to go."

Alicia went ahead and took the woman up on the generous offer, just as more and more big, fat raindrops began to fall in earnest. As much as Alicia wanted to know the kindly woman's name, she couldn't seem to introduce herself and didn't expect the woman to do so, either. However, the woman did ask Alicia where she needed to go and afterward appeared perfectly content to drive in total silence. Alicia was hardly sociable, but even she was disappointed. Nonetheless, she didn't take it personally, as the woman smiled the entire duration.

At the office, Alicia turned up the heat, not only to warm herself but to dry her jacket in preparation for the walk home—after picking up "the ring" at the jewelry store. If the weather became too awful, she might call Vance and ask if he could give her a ride home.

All this could have been avoided if she would have driven herself to work.

By afternoon, Alicia had a sniffle and a sore throat. She hadn't bothered to bring lunch, but she wasn't hungry, anyway. Fortunately there was bottled water in the refrigerator in the back. Even better, she had the office to herself. Then again, it wouldn't have been the worst thing to ask Mr. Brewer or Jill for a ride home, should Vance not be available. Other than a couple calls from solicitors, the phone didn't ring all day.

Quitting time couldn't come soon enough, and Alicia even dared to close the office a few minutes early so she could make her trek to the jewelry store and pick up the ring. It hadn't snowed yet but was sleeting by this time, and the wind had increased, blowing almost incessantly. Although her jacket had dried, it was soaking wet by the time she reached Fitzpatrick's. The clerk who waited on her wasn't the owner, Jim, who was a bit overbearing. Nonetheless, Alicia still didn't have the nerve to tell the guy it wasn't necessary for her to try on the ring because it wasn't going to be hers, anyway.

Naturally the ring fit perfectly. It looked so beautiful, Alicia couldn't help tearing up. Not only that, she wore the ring for the long, wet, dark walk home. Despite barely being able to see the ring, she kept glancing at it, unable to believe it was actually on her finger. As soon as she got home, however, she'd get in her car and take the ring to Vance's.

There was a crosswalk Alicia used, to navigate always busy Route 36, as she would never jaywalk, increasing the chances of getting hit by a vehicle. Anymore, she always second guessed herself, so she had to be extra careful.

Alicia was about to look one last time and cross the road, when on the other side, under a streetlight, there was a young girl waving at her, whose face appeared to resemble Claudia's! She was wearing a long white dress with a waist-length black cape, the hood over her head. Was it possible the horrendous event that stole Claudia's and Troy's lives was all in Alicia's imagination?

Since Alicia couldn't discern what color the girl's hair was, it was imperative she cross the road immediately and confirm up close if it was her daughter. The second she was halfway across, she could see the girl was none other than Angeline, who was suddenly pointing and laughing!

Meanwhile, an empty livestock tractor-trailer happened to be rapidly approaching from Alicia's left, and the driver was unprepared to stop, although he never even saw Alicia; all he knew was it felt like the truck went over a speed bump on one side. Having driven the route hundreds of times, that much was doubtful but he kept going anyway, not wanting to waste his time stopping.

Who Says Real Estate Is Boring?

It was a small wonder Nellie Matthews' father filed for divorce from her mother, Midge, before his daughter reached her sixth birthday. As Nellie grew up, she became increasingly aware it wasn't something to take personally, despite the fact he never even made an effort to see her. At this point he was probably dead.

Nowadays Nellie was working for her mother, which was probably going to be temporary. As an "independent contractor," Nellie was formerly employed as a broker associate at "Lake View Realty" in Ogden Dunes, Indiana. Out of the blue her mother had called and begged Nellie to come work at her "M. M. Real Estate." Since Nellie was answering the phone at Lake View and not doing much else, she couldn't tell her mother "no." It was tempting to do so, however. The two hadn't even spoken to one another for close to two years, following an argument about something or the other. (Nellie honestly couldn't recall what it was about.)

The real shocker was this morning Nellie's mother left for a four-day vacation in Honolulu, and Midge hated taking time off. She was obsessed with the real estate business and all that it entailed. Before leaving for the airport, Midge told her daughter, "In this business, no two days are alike, and you never know what you'll come upon!"

Nellie was willing to agree with her mother's declaration, despite having very limited exposure to any real estate transactions. Hopefully that would change while she ran M.M. Real Estate singlehandedly while her mother was away.

It-Girl and Other Stories

Nellie was allowed to take any leads that came her way, versus having to turn them over to her mother when she returned.

M.M. Real Estate was located in a quaint section of Michigan City, Indiana, where several turn-of-the-century houses had been converted into businesses. The one in which the real estate office was located, was wedged between a coffee shop and a chocolatier. Lake View Realty was closer to Lake Michigan, in a building that also housed a mortgage company and a title company.

Nellie's mother had never been lovable, it was safe to say. Overall, Midge wasn't a bad person, however, so Nellie forgave her. That and the fact Nellie needed to make something of her real estate career, was why she "switched offices." Also, Midge's only other broker, Corrine Jesper, recently retired. Nellie needed one good sale and her mother might actually respect her.

Nellie got into real estate because her mother told her she didn't have what it took, a dare if there ever was one. Nellie had tried several other careers, only to find herself restless and bored. Once she had her real estate license, it never occurred to her, to work at her mother's office. Why put herself through hell? At the same time, she was aware working at Lake View would be so competitive she wouldn't even be in the running – and she was right!

The worst part of Nellie's relationship with her mother was when they hadn't been communicating at all with one another, amazingly enough. Nellie hadn't fully realized as much until her mother reached out to her in regard to moving to M.M. Real Estate. Golden opportunity though it was, Nellie could not let go of her suspicion something was up, especially given the other circumstances. Nonetheless Nellie was here at the office on Monday morning, ready to take calls. She would also have calls forwarded to her cell phone if she had to leave to show one of her mother's listings.

It was possible Nellie's mother had a lover she was meeting in Hawaii (or even meeting him at the airport). As far as Nellie was aware, however, her mother hadn't been in a relationship since her husband left her two decades ago! That was sad in a way, but she kind of deserved it, given how hurtful and hateful she could be, all the while oblivious. Maybe the trip would give her mother some perspective.

Just after nine, Nellie got her first call. After saying, "M.M. Real Estate, this is Nellie. Can I help you?" She was asked if Midge Matthews was available, to which she replied, "No. She's out of town for a few days."

The woman sarcastically remarked, "Great. I'll call back next week and maybe the bitch will finally be around."

Nellie tried to hang up before the irate client/customer did, but she wasn't quick enough. Thankfully she had a pretty thick skin—courtesy of none other than her mother.

Morgan Fletcher was having trouble finding a suitable property for one of her clients. It seemed as if the perfect place was eluding Morgan, and she refused to believe her client was unreasonable, not when the client had the financial means to look at properties in the three million dollar range. However, thanks to Morgan's unwavering determination she managed to find a listing this morning, that appeared to be just what her client was looking for. It had been on the market for almost ninety days, which wasn't long at all for an upscale property on Lake Michigan. Morgan had decided on a whim to type in four million for the top listing price, thinking maybe there was a seller sufficiently motivated to drop half a million or more to get closer to the three range. Morgan had been in the real estate business for twenty-five years and really knew her stuff. The only one in the area who maybe was more knowledgeable was her sister, Clarisse. She was the managing broker/owner of "Home Of Your Dreams Realty," in Michiana Shores, Indiana, close to the Michigan state line. Morgan too was a broker there.

The client, Jocelyn Helstrom, wasn't actually the one

buying the property. Her soon-to-be ex-husband, Michael, was (and he was paying cash). His livelihood necessitated he have a condominium in downtown Chicago, and he spent most of his time there. Nonetheless, he still wanted the Lake Michigan house Jocelyn and he shared with their two children. Since Jocelyn intended to remain in the area he offered to buy her a house. Whatever the couple's reasons for divorcing, Mr. Helstrom obviously wanted his ex-wife to be happy.

Thus far, Morgan had shown Jocelyn several properties, not all of them on the lakefront, as she had been willing to keep an open mind about possible living arrangements. The two had met several times at Home Of Your Dreams' office, which was located in a split-log "house" on Route 12. It was Morgan's pet project decorating it, as she briefly had a career in interior design before getting into real estate. Evidently Jocelyn enjoyed stopping by to go over listings, as she preferred they not simply be e-mailed to her. Morgan would serve coffee, and fresh pastries were always available. While discussing the listings the two inevitably started talking about other topics, such as restaurants worth visiting in the area as well as other places, including Chicago. Morgan's husband, Grant, worked downtown too, but he came home every night, unlike Mr. Helstrom. (Grant and Morgan had been married for close to three decades.)

Morgan went ahead and called M.M. Real Estate's office number, as that was the company with the listing. Midge Matthews was the owner and was currently the only one working there, Morgan was almost certain. Her one associate broker, Corrine Jesper, recently retired, and there were few brokers willing to put up with how "difficult" Midge could be, which was to say she was often times overly-blunt. Morgan had to admit, however, if Midge Matthews was part of a transaction, it was a sure bet it would close. At the same time, that wasn't to say there might not be some bumps in the road.

It turned out Nellie Matthews, Midge's daughter,

answered. She was formerly at Lake View, which was a madhouse. There were too many agents, yet the same ones got all the business. It was the office to work in if you wanted to kill your new real estate career.

Morgan hadn't expected Nellie to be well-acquainted with the property in question, but it turned out her mother must have thoroughly educated her on it. Not only that, Nellie sounded articulate and engaging. Better yet, Morgan liked everything she was told about the house, so she set up a showing appointment for the following day, assuming Ms. Helstrom would be available. She pretty much was during school hours, as she had two kids in elementary school. They took the bus in the morning, but she usually picked them up after school. If the appointment time wouldn't work, Morgan told Nellie, she'd call back and reschedule.

Midge had a hard time going along with someone when he or she was hiding something, including a client who had an upscale listing, such as Mr. Lester Nadell. Recently there was an incident involving his house and what Midge was certain was a dead body in the library. It was literally all she could think about, precipitating the need to leave town for a few days, to clear her head. Otherwise it was almost impossible to tear herself away from her real estate business. It brought out her competitiveness, which she realized was what made her appear aggressive or even rude.

For the duration of time Midge was away, she left M.M. Real Estate in the hands of her daughter, Nellie, who'd recently started working for the company. Midge hated to admit she begged Nellie to join her, but it was true. At the same time Midge liked to think Nellie was relieved to be on board, as she wasn't getting anywhere career-wise, where she worked before. (Midge refused to name the real estate office because it was free advertising.) As it was, Midge wanted to show Nellie the real estate ropes, and her daughter would be exposed to more situations if she worked at M.M. Real Estate. Given what Midge had been through lately, the latter couldn't have been more accurate.

Fortunately Midge had an aisle seat for the flight to Honolulu. As soon as the plane took off, the pilot welcomed everyone and stated the final cruising altitude, etc. Midge barely paid any attention because she was busy marveling at how the stranger to her right not only fell asleep before take-off but remained so in the interim – and still was. It wasn't as if she'd wanted someone with whom to chat; she just wondered what he took to put him out so quickly.

A dead woman was in the library of Mr. Nadell's, there was no denying it! Midge could hardly think about anything else, hence she had to bring it up again. The woman might have been Mr. Nadell's live-in housekeeper; it seemed like every time Midge was at the house, he had new help. He was probably extremely exacting, which made Midge wonder if her days as his real estate agent were numbered. The listing agreement was for a year, but he could terminate it at any time.

As of the past couple weeks, Mr. Nadell had another resident besides whoever his latest housekeeper was: his nephew, Alex. He was around more than his uncle was. Mr. Nadell traveled often for both business and pleasure. That was one reason he was selling his lakefront house. Also, with a spacious penthouse apartment in downtown Chicago, within walking distance to his office as well as shopping, entertainment and cultural destinations, he preferred city life. Most importantly, having become a widower two years ago, he gave himself that time to grieve and then decided to make some changes. His wife, Rena, loved their Lake Michigan house, but it was time to say good-bye. However, Mr. Nadell made it clear to Midge he was in no hurry to sell and didn't intend to take less than the full list price (four million). Midge couldn't resist computing what half the four percent commission would be. In this case she would be happy to split it with the selling agent. With some transactions it seemed like she did all the work, especially if she was the one with the listing.

Regarding Alex, Midge didn't even know his last name because he was the son of Mr. Nadell's sister (and she didn't even know that woman's first name). Supposedly Alex was without a job and a place to live, which sounded like a little too much bad luck hurled at him at once. In other words, he might be a bum. Nonetheless, he was very attractive and overly solicitous, compelling Midge to feel sorry for him and give him the benefit of the doubt. Simultaneously, when she was around him she felt very uncomfortable, afraid, even.

Midge had been so undone by seeing the woman lying on the wood floor of the library, she'd determined to exit the residence. Once she reached her car, she'd call her clients and cancel on them, claiming she was suddenly very ill. As it was, how could she be expected to show a house with a dead body in one of the rooms?

As Midge had made her way to the front door, who should be in the gray marble foyer but Mr. Nadell, rifling through the closet that was under the staircase. She thought he'd already left for the day, as he'd said he had a business meeting downtown and was staying there overnight. It was imperative she get his attention without startling him, so she tried to clear her throat without sounding obnoxious about it. When he turned around, Midge skipped any sort of greeting and nervously said, "Mr. Nadell, I need you to come look at something." She couldn't say what "it" was because she remained incredulous about the whole situation.

Mr. Nadell backed out of the closet and obediently followed Midge to the library, where the door was closed—and she swore it had been open. Right inside the doorway was Alex, looking very indignant. Managing to peer around him, there was no longer a body to be seen. As much as Midge wanted to ask him what he did with it, she couldn't. The presence of these two men, both of them handsome but austere-looking, was overwhelming. Her usual nerve had obviously deserted her.

Alex spoke first (while glaring at Midge): "Uncle Lester, I have to have a word with you in private, if you don't mind."

The showing was still on, after all. Midge didn't want to come upon any more dead bodies. That was her only request.

Yesterday morning, Jocelyn got a call from her real estate agent, Morgan Fletcher, informing her that an appointment had been made to look at a house today, at noon. Usually that time was fine, as it was understood Jocelyn was essentially available from about nine until two-thirty on school days. The "problem" was Jocelyn had acquired a lover in the past week. Already she'd fantasized about marrying him, yet her divorce wasn't even final. She was actually the one holding it up because of her inability to settle on a suitable property for her kids and herself. She was willing to live close to Lake Michigan, versus right on it, but the house would have to be as spectacular as the one she was letting her soon-to-be ex-husband have.

Although Jocelyn initiated the divorce proceedings because she was sick of her husband, Michael, being more married to his job than he was to her (his lengthy absences were killing her), he was almost too eager to agree to end their union. Jocelyn never thought of the situation like that before; she'd been grateful to have had an amicable divorce thus far.

Jocelyn's lover, Alex, was a man she barely knew, including his last name. She'd met him at "Healthy-U" gym, where she'd started going after separating from her husband. Her thinking had been, if she ever wanted to get married again, she'd better look more fit than she did. Nor did she have any intention of being a fat divorcee. Alex had purposely bumped into her as she was leaving the gym after a workout, and she'd loved his "nerve." Of course she accepted his invite to have a drink with him at the juice bar. It didn't take long for things to progress from there. It was so unlike her! All she could conclude was she was so starved for affection and sexual satisfaction, thanks to Michael's ongoing absences, she finally lost her moral standard. And this youngish hunk had plenty of endurance, but Jocelyn had no trouble keeping up. Married to Michael, she'd thought her libido had died.

Alex hadn't been notified Jocelyn had an appointment to look at a house later until he tried to get her interested in yet another round of lovemaking (and she resisted). He was visibly annoyed but managed to slip in a couple of kisses before she slid out of his grasp and got up. She wasn't at all self-conscious and knew she looked great from behind, even (or especially?) naked. Hopefully Alex wanted her so badly he couldn't stand it, which really turned her on.

Meanwhile, Alex was going to play coy with this "hot older woman" he couldn't seem to get enough of. It was almost impossible to keep his hands off her. He felt like he was saving the day, giving her something she'd been missing in a sexless marriage. She refused to tell him her age, and he had yet to tell her much of anything about himself, including his last name. Alex had been around enough to know not to tell a woman much unless you were like super, intensely interested in her. Actually he was in this case, but he didn't want to let on about as much, not yet. He was in absolutely no hurry to be tied down. And Jocelyn had two kids. Alex was starting to realize how quickly things could get complicated when you screwed a woman who was "getting a divorce." One holdup was the fact she couldn't find a house she liked. Her ex was taking the house they had currently, and the dummy was buying her another place! Alex would have kicked her to the curb and told her to f**k herself.

Elbows propping him up, Alex attempted to keep watching Jocelyn as she picked out an outfit before getting in the shower. Even though she wasn't a "career woman," the fact she had two kids made her life as structured as any CEO's. He was closer to knowing about as much than one would have assumed, thanks to his uncle Lester.

At the expense of pissing off a woman Alex honestly did not want to (a new one for him), he left Jocelyn's before she emerged from the shower. It was evident as hell she had no intention of reappearing before she was dressed and ready for her goddamned appointment. That was fine with him; he figured if he played hard to get (and keep) she would fall all over herself to have him, just the way he wanted it (and what he was accustomed to).

One thing Alex had been brought up to believe was arrogance was a virtue. Both his parents thought like that, and both were exceptionally good-looking, so he had physical attractiveness going for him, too. He couldn't have lived with himself, otherwise.

Jocelyn hadn't wanted to be late for the appointment to see the house her real estate agent found for her, but it looked like she would be, by a few minutes. Her lover ended up ambushing her when she'd emerged from the shower. After their "quickie" he confessed to having left while she was showering but had returned because he didn't want her to take his departure "the wrong way." That sounded like repentance, which was a real turn-on. If Jocelyn's husband had any idea she had a lover in their bed, he would not be pleased at all. Michael did have plenty of pride. It wasn't possible he had a girlfriend who shared his place in Chicago because all he cared about was working! It was highly doubtful he'd just show up while Alex and Jocelyn were in bed, as he had accepted the fact they were finished. Alex could sneak over just about any time because he supposedly lived rather close by and walked here. Rather than find that troubling (as in maybe he had a DUI), Jocelyn considered as much "quaint." She never thought deeply enough to consider if he had some sort of employment.

The house Jocelyn was supposed to look at was only about a mile and a half from her and Michael's current place, both on Lake Shore Drive, overlooking Lake Michigan. From

Amy Kristoff

what Jocelyn had been told about the property, it was everything she was looking for. The biggest issue was the price—four million. Michael had explicitly told her not to pick something out that was too much over three (million).

Pulling into the driveway of what was potentially her and her kids' new home, Jocelyn liked it already, with the stone around the front and encircling the arched entryway, leading to an oversized front door that resembled a barn door, as did each door on the three-car garage. The overall design resembled a very classy, modernistic farmhouse, its bonus the fact it was on Lake Michigan. Did she mention she already liked it? There was also a wide, concrete parking area to the right of the house, providing extra room for guests to park when she threw her intimate but fabulous dinner parties (no more than two couples). Realistically, however, now that she would be single again, she might lose some of her and Michael's friends. It was a safe bet none of them would approve of Alex.

If the design of the house didn't sound like something that was "appropriate" for a property on Lake Michigan, you had to see it to realize how well-suited it was. The question was, what kind of person would live in a house with so much character? Did Jocelyn even belong here? Michael was proud of the fact their house was impersonal-looking, with exterior support beams, a flat roof and narrow windows.

Morgan sighed with relief when Jocelyn Helstrom's white Mercedes pulled into the driveway of the house of her dreams (hopefully, anyway). However, Ms. Helstrom proceeded to remain in her car, talking on her phone. She wasn't late, but Morgan was very anxious about this showing and wanted to get moving. Although Morgan had done plenty of "big deals," this one definitely qualified as the biggest. Nonetheless, if any agent could handle the responsibility, it was her.

Having already briefly previewed some of the house while she was waiting for Ms. Helstrom, Morgan noticed there was stainless everything in the kitchen, professional-grade, and it just so happened Ms. Helstrom liked to cook when she had the leisure of some free time. That should sell the house right there. As it was, Morgan anticipated an enjoyable showing because she'd requested no one be present but the listing agent. In this case it was Nellie Matthews, standing in for her mother, Midge. Nellie didn't need to be here, but the seller required her presence. She had parked her car in the street, although there wasn't much room, as Lake Shore Drive wasn't very wide. Luckily she drove a MINI Cooper.

Jocelyn never thought she would be "high" on a house, but she was in regard to the one she looked at earlier today. Even though she wanted to tell her Realtor she'd "take it," Michael insisted she "sleep on it" and look at it one more time. She felt like a child, forced to temper herself. In the morning she'd call Morgan Fletcher and ask to see the house again. Then she'd make an offer (supposedly the seller wasn't going to take a "lowball" offer) and tell Michael to start putting the money together. She needed to be grateful he was letting her buy a house that was much more money than he'd intended to spend.

As far as Alex, Jocelyn wished she could talk to him about more things. Actually she wished she could talk to him about something, anything! Michael never communicated much because he was always on the go, while Alex only had one thing on his mind. To top it off, she could already tell he had a hair-trigger temper. He had yet to totally "lose it" with her, but that was inevitable. The fact he was so different from Michael was intriguing – for the time being.

Dinner tonight was Chef Boyardee Spaghetti and Meatballs, and Jocelyn was stirring it in a pan on the stove. The landline phone rang, and she used the cordless handset to answer the call. It was her Realtor, Morgan Fletcher. Pleasantries exchanged, Morgan wanted to know if Jocelyn had any questions about the house or did she want to see it again?

Jocelyn told Morgan she "had to" see it again, not elaborating. Then Jocelyn's daughter, Cristina, interrupted the conversation by asking, "Why do we suddenly never have real dinners anymore?"

"Shh! I'm on the phone!" Jocelyn replied, infuriated by the distraction, not to mention the fact there wasn't an answer to give that wasn't too revealing. It was time-consuming having a lover! She'd cook elaborate meals again when Alex and she "simmered down," so to speak. Meanwhile, Jocelyn told Morgan, "Sorry about that." However, given the commission Morgan stood to make on the sale, no apology was really necessary. Nonetheless, thanks to Jocelyn's superior upbringing, she was always gracious. And her daughter was expected to be a carbon copy of herself.

It was decided between the two women, Morgan would call Jocelyn when it had been confirmed with Nellie Matthews, the time for the second showing. Jocelyn pretended to be available during the day, but currently her life revolved around when Alex wanted her. Still, her kids were her top priority.

Speaking of them, Jocelyn could hardly wait to finish the call so she could deliver a diatribe to her ungrateful daughter, with her son listening too: "Cristina, please just sit down and wait for dinner to be ready, no matter what the hell it is, got it? Aaron's been at his place all this time, keeping quiet, why can't you? You need to have more patience." And Jocelyn was a hypocrite because she had no patience at all.

As if on cue, from the "safety" of the far corner of the dining nook in the kitchen, Aaron asked why they had to leave this house and move down the street.

Jocelyn put off her son's question by saying, "I'll tell you after we eat." Even she was starving by this time. She wished Alex would call her just to say "hi," nothing extravagant. Doing so would help convince her he was interested in her for more than just sex.

Barely had Jocelyn served the spaghetti and meatball dinner when Aaron had the nerve to next ask, "Will Dad ever live with us again?" As much as he'd wanted to keep that question to himself and just see what happened, he couldn't help it! He had so many questions right now, he was ready to burst. Upon first finding out his parents were divorcing, Aaron was upset, but more and more, he was glad. It would stop his mom from complaining about him working too much and never being home "when she needed him," which she used to say a lot. Lately she hadn't said it at all, and Dad had been living at his place downtown. He was avoiding her because she was mean to him, even when they were supposed to be together! If Aaron had things his way, he'd eliminate his sister, Cristina, from the picture. He loved her but could live without her. Mom would be super-mad at him for even thinking that, while Dad would just laugh.

    Nellie got a call about ten Thursday morning from Morgan Fletcher with this news: "If you haven't gotten the O.K. from your client yet to show the house at noon, so much the better. I just received a call from my client, and she's prepared to make a full-price offer and has her proof of funds letter and the earnest money check in hand! She's stopping by my office in about an hour to sign the purchase agreement, and I will email you everything. Her ex requires she have the house inspected, since she's skipping the second showing. And she already made the appointment, which happens to be at noon! I hope this isn't moving too fast for you, Nellie!"
    Truth be told, Nellie wanted to catch her breath and enjoy some of this. She had been about to call Morgan and give her the go-ahead for the noon showing. It had taken Nellie from last evening until just now, to get ahold of Mr. Nadell. He offered no excuse but did say he was driving back from the city while he was on the phone with her. Hopefully she could get ahold of him again soon because he needed to be apprised of these late-breaking developments. Also, it would be necessary for him to sign the purchase agreement.

Amy Kristoff

As it was he said he would be present for the second showing, and Nellie didn't see a problem with that. Instead there would be a whole house inspection. That stood to be interesting. Not everyone stuck around for those, including the agents, but this wasn't just any property.

Sure enough, Morgan indicated her buyer intended to be present "because her ex-husband told her to." However, Morgan claimed she had some things come up and might not be there until close to the end. Nellie figured since the listing might go from "Contingent on Inspection" to "Pending" within the span of a few hours, Morgan was already onto something else. The only issue that could put the brakes on the property closing, was the buyer reconciling with her soon-to- be ex-husband. Or so it appeared.

At eleven in the morning, Jocelyn went to her Realtor's office. It was in a log cabin-style building, surrounded by tall pines, appropriately enough. The reception area had a rust-colored, overstuffed leather sofa and two matching armchairs, complementing the earth-toned, striped rug that covered a large portion of the wide-plank wood floor. Various real estate-related magazines and brochures were scattered on the rough-hewn wood coffee table.

Morgan was not immediately available to see Jocelyn, providing an opportunity for Jocelyn to enjoy the comfort of one of the armchairs. The receptionist asked her if she would like a cup of coffee, but she declined. She was too excited about her new house to need any more caffeine than she already had this morning. It was easy to forget all this was necessary only because she was divorcing Michael. It wasn't like she hated him; she simply could no longer stand feeling like she was single while very much a married woman. Once she and the kids got settled in the new house, she promised to spend more time with them. Before that, however, she needed to make sure she finally had Alex's complete, undivided attention (if that was even possible).

It-Girl and Other Stories

***

Nellie arrived a few minutes early for the inspection of Mr. Nadell's house. Fortunately she'd been able to get ahold of him right after she spoke with Morgan Fletcher. He sounded pleased to hear the buyer was making a full price offer, and he signed the purchase agreement when she'd emailed it to him about thirty minutes ago. Provided there were no major problems with the house, the transaction appeared destined to sail right through. She even got a call from the inspector, confirming the address. He'd gotten her number from the listing, although the buyer had made the appointment.

Mr. Nadell opened the front door when Nellie knocked on it, looking spiffy in a royal blue, long-sleeved oxford shirt, pleated khakis and brown leather loafers. He greeted her and indicated for her to step inside. She wanted to ask him, "Are we alone?" so there wouldn't be any surprises when she moved around the house, opening shades and shutters, turning on light switches, etc. Then she remembered she was here for the inspection and didn't have to stage anything. She couldn't help wondering where Mr. Nadell's nephew, Alex, was. What little Nellie knew about him, was thanks to what her mother revealed. And she hadn't exactly portrayed him in a positive light.

Nellie certainly didn't expect to get any information about Alex out of his uncle. If Mr. Nadell spoke, you listened, and that was that. He proceeded to mention he'd be "in the back for the time being" and would be around at some point after the inspector and buyer showed up.

No sooner did Mr. Nadell disappear when a car door was slammed out front and then another, shortly thereafter. Nellie peered out a porthole window by the stairway to see Ms. Helstrom in a "deep embrace" with a tall, muscular-looking man with thick, wavy, dark brown hair, by the driver's side door of her Mercedes. Given the way they were pressed together, the guy couldn't have been her estranged husband.

Amy Kristoff

After the two lovebirds made out for half a minute (and Nellie shamelessly witnessed the whole thing), Ms. Helstrom started walking toward the front door but was abruptly stopped. Her lover had grabbed her right arm and wasn't exactly delicate about it. He also pointed at her car, making it clear he wanted them to leave again. Nellie couldn't help but have a sinking feeling, aware how tenuous this sale really was.

Ms. Helstrom must have won the argument because soon she approached the front doorway and was even heard laughing. A few seconds later, her lover joined her. Nellie opened the door and before she could even greet the couple, Ms. Helstrom exclaimed, "Alex's uncle owns this place! Alex has even lived here occasionally. Doesn't that prove once and for all it's a small world? I love it!"

Meanwhile, Alex looked anything but pleased about the situation and wanted nothing more than to bolt. Nellie then noticed the death grip Ms. Helstrom had on Alex's hand. Even so, she acted like everything was fine and asked Nellie, "Is the inspector here yet?"

"He should be any minute," Nellie replied. Two seconds later, she received a text from none other than Dale Ross of "Ross House Inspections": "I am here and will be doing an exterior inspection before needing access to the interior. Thanks. D."

While Nellie had been distracted by her phone, the two lovers ascended the stairs. She wouldn't have immediately guessed as much, except she suddenly heard a loud thud from above. Alex started shouting something unintelligible (and most likely unprintable), and Ms. Helstrom sounded like she was trying to "shush" him. It wasn't working.

Alex next descended the stairs, saying, "You set me up, you damned bitch! I tried to believe you were clueless about the whole situation and everything would blow over, but no. Uncle Lester must have put you up to this. You two probably have a thing going, to top it off. Is he a better fuck than me?

It-Girl and Other Stories

Huh?"

"I have no idea what or who you're talking about!" Ms. Helstrom exclaimed as she followed her lover down the stairs.

"Oh, sure," Alex remarked, his voice dripping with sarcasm. "Plead ignorance when it suits your pretty little self."

Nellie had been standing to the side of the stairway, just out of the line of sight of the two quarreling lovers, not that either one appeared to be aware of much besides each other —but not in a good way at the moment. She moved closer to the side, so she could be even more out of the way and practically hidden from view by an oak column. The last thing she needed was to be blamed for eavesdropping on their argument.

By this time Alex was at the bottom of the stairs and Ms. Helstrom was one step above him. He turned to face her while clenching and unclenching his fists. Nellie gave Ms. Helstrom credit for standing her ground while Alex looked ready to literally strangle her.

Both turned their heads when the inspector passed by the five floor-to-ceiling windows to their right, on the other side of the sunken alcove that was a cozy sitting area. He was on the deck, looking around while talking into a small, handheld recorder. Alex proceeded to grab Jocelyn's elbows and shake her, demanding to know, "Are you still expecting to get a confession out of me? Is that it? 'Cause it looks like the place might be surrounded! O.K., here it is . . . I didn't kill her on purpose. It was an accident! I choked her to shut her up."

When it appeared as if Jocelyn was too shocked to have even heard Alex, he stopped shaking her and repeated, "It was an accident, do you hear me? You need to because no one is going to believe me. I need you to believe that for me!" Then he began to sob!

Nellie never imagined this particular house inspection would be mundane, so she wasn't surprised on that count.

51

However, they weren't supposed to be filled with high drama, like this one was. At least she didn't get too far ahead of herself by assuming the house would be a breeze to close on.

"Out of nowhere" Mr. Nadell appeared, evidently having heard what his nephew just said. His sudden presence surprised Alex, who looked ready to make a run for it. In the meantime, his uncle declared, "Your time is up, Alex. You'd previously told me you found Fatima lying there in the library and had seen her using drugs on occasion. I actually believed you and I'm not sure why. I had to call my lawyer and make him the responsible party in making sure she was taken to the hospital and he signed off on everything. I shouldn't even be bringing this up right now because there could still be legal repercussions. You definitely will require some legal counsel."

"Could you call your lawyer for me, Uncle Lester?" Alex implored.

"I can't and won't. I've done more than enough for you and how do you repay me but strangle the housekeeper!"

"I didn't like her rejecting me."

"Jeez. I cannot believe I'm even having this conversation."

"I'm outta here," Alex said, heading for the front door. "I always got a ton of lectures from my mom, who's your fucking sister . . . It never did me any good. I don't need this shit."

Mr. Nadell glared at his nephew while watching him depart. Ms. Helstrom kept her eyes focused on Alex until he disappeared outside and then looked at Lester Nadell. Somehow she couldn't look away and didn't mind appearing rude.

"And you are?" Lester Nadell asked Jocelyn, stepping forward to introduce himself and shake hands.

"Jocelyn Helstrom."

"Lester Nadell," he said. "It's an honor to meet you." Then he shook hands with his new acquaintance and added, "I must apologize for my nephew's foul language, as I find as much intolerable, particularly in polite company. Whatever relationship you have with him is none of my business, but he's a bad egg, as it turns out. At this point, out of sight, out of mind."

"He arrived with me and doesn't have a ride otherwise," Jocelyn said, sounding nervous because she was! It was hell feeling inferior to someone. "So unless he knows how to hotwire my Mercedes, it's going to take him a long time to get anywhere."

Surprising everyone, there was a tap on the front door and it flew open. Dale Ross, the inspector, walked in, looking very upset. He said, "This guy came out of the house and started to leave on foot until he saw me on the roof. He threw my ladder on the ground and got in my truck. I always leave a key in it. So he started it and left, just like it was his. I went to the back of the house and slid down, holding onto the downspout in the corner, by the kitchen. Thanks to the deck, the landing wasn't hard."

Mr. Nadell mumbled, "I'm going to have lawsuits up the wazoo before this is over. I should have just kept this place and been done with it. It's not like I need the money. I think I'm just trying to erase my lingering grief from losing my wife Rena."

"I'm so sorry," Jocelyn said and couldn't wait to give Mr. Nadell a hug. The way he reciprocated the gesture, it was safe to say the two would soon have something going together!

Nellie was sincerely happy for the new couple and didn't even care if the deal fell through. It was proof she was only out for a client's best interests, how any Realtor should be.

Who Is the Selfish One?

"Bye, Daddy, see you tonight," little Darlene Havelin told her father, Chad, as he waved and then backed his white Toyota Camry (a company car) out of the garage Monday morning. His wife, Stephanie, used to stand in the garage doorway and say good-bye too, but anymore she stayed in the kitchen, cleaning up after breakfast. Chad didn't want to "get after her," because she was a good mother overall, but he thought their daughter still needed supervision while he was "in transit."

Stephanie unfailingly accompanied Darlene to the bus stop, which was at the end of the street, Primrose. That also happened to be where the mailboxes were located. This particular subdivision in Scottsdale, Arizona, "Turquoise Estates," was rather upscale, so perhaps the developer thought having the mail delivered to a central place added to the subdivision's sophistication. (Chad liked to think that, anyway.)

Whatever the case, the large, metal, free-standing mailbox stand provided a common area for the neighbors, as they otherwise would have little opportunity to see one another. Stephanie had yet to make friends with a single neighbor, although she did exchange "hellos" with some of the mothers when she walked Darlene to the bus stop. The mailbox stand also had flyers posted on it from time to time, and the postal carrier didn't appear to mind. As of late there was one offering babysitting services. Chad always picked up the mail after work, stopping his car at the stand. It was only about a hundred yards from their house, so it wasn't far to walk to, either.

Stephanie's only friend was Micaela Cutler. The two had known one another from their college days, in Ohio. Micaela had moved to Phoenix from Toledo with her husband because of his job, just like Stephanie did with Chad (along with Darlene, who was barely a year old at the time). He had been transferred to Arizona by "Quiet Golf Car Company," originally based in Toledo. Fortunately Stephanie immediately took to the desert climate and new environment, or Chad wouldn't have known what to do. Everything with her was always so tenuous, and it was impossible to predict what might upset her. Married to her for close to ten years, he still considered her an enigma.

Chad's weekday morning commute was about twenty-five minutes to QGCC's relocated headquarters, just off the 101 Freeway, in Mesa. Even though he was high enough on the corporate totem pole it wasn't necessary to punch a time clock, he made sure to arrive by eight-thirty. Maybe he was so used to being punctual he couldn't help himself, was all.

Chad was patiently waiting for a raise and/or a promotion. The problem was he had a co-worker, Carl Dante, with the exact same expectation(s). Carl happened to be on vacation the whole week, and Chad had a hunch their boss, Leonard Ganin, was going to make his decision in the meantime. The "good part" was at least Carl and Chad got along, although that possibly wouldn't be for much longer.

An issue the two QGCC executives had agreed on was the possibility their eccentric boss would find a way to test one or both of them. Whatever the test entailed, it would have nothing to do with their positions at the company. Since Carl was on vacation, Chad feared he would be made the initial target. If Mr. Ganin didn't like how Chad reacted to what he was forced to do, he might give Carl the raise and promotion instead!

Chad didn't have a week off for another month, at the

same time as Darlene's spring break, in mid-March. Stephanie had made plans for them to go to Disneyland for some of it. The remainder of Chad's week off, he planned on being at Stephanie's beck and call, which he actually enjoyed. It made up for the fact he worked long hours and wasn't home as much as he would have liked. Although she never complained about being lonely, he wondered if she was. Making friends wasn't easy for her, and she detested social media. One positive aspect to that was Darlene wouldn't be getting a cell phone anytime soon.

Even if Stephanie had no neighbors she was friends with, she did have Micaela Cutler. Chad frankly didn't like her and was ashamed for thinking like that. It was fortunate Stephanie never suggested they go out with Micaela and her husband, Vince. He was a software developer, which made him sound super-smart. So how did he marry Micaela? That was Chad's "inside joke," since he could never share it with anyone, definitely not Stephanie.

Unlike some, Stephanie preferred Monday over every other day of the week. Even when she was employed full-time, back "home" in Toledo, she felt that way, no matter what employment she had. Nonetheless, she was proud to say she was currently a stay-at-home wife and mother and felt as much or more satisfaction with her life than when she worked. The social aspect of employment had always been a strain, and her daily life nowadays offered a sanctuary, despite how her situation might appear. Chad, her husband, seemed to enjoy being the sole breadwinner, and his executive position at a golf cart manufacturing company, paid very well. The subdivision where they lived, proved it. Most importantly, their daughter, Darlene, seemed to like the fact Mommy was always available to walk her to the bus stop in the morning and was waiting for her when she returned from school. Sometimes Stephanie wished this time in her life would never change, and her seven-year-old daughter would always be young and needy (in a good way).

Monday was Stephanie's "major housecleaning day," and she wore grubby clothes for it, to do plenty of scrubbing, dusting and vacuuming. Chad positively loathed the sound of the vacuum, so it was pure joy to vacuum when he wasn't home. Funnily enough, back when they had just married and were still living in Toledo, the sound of the vacuum was a non-issue. It made Stephanie wonder exactly how satisfied Chad was with having relocated here. He worked as many hours as he did because he "had to," but she couldn't figure out if he was satisfying a personal quota or his boss'. If Chad truthfully didn't have to work as much as he did, he deserved to be promoted for that reason alone.

Chad happened to be very good at not noticing anything, which was really starting to grate on Stephanie's nerves. Surprise, surprise, he had always been like that. His wake-up call would be in the form of getting passed over for a promotion/raise. Maybe then he'd finally spend more quality time with his family, rather than falling asleep in front of the TV every evening because he overworked himself for no good reason.

Ironically, Chad worked for a golf car company, yet he couldn't play the game itself and even hated it (which didn't help matters insofar as him trying to improve his horrible swing). His job was in crunching numbers and helping the company turn a profit, but it was still ironic he couldn't play the game worth a whit. What was outright funny was the fact he had to play in the company golf tournament this weekend, having been allowed to bow out in prior years.

There was a time (the duration of which was about a millisecond) when Stephanie was seriously contemplating getting pregnant again. Darlene had just turned four, and Stephanie was so proud of her, she was inspired. However, Chad immediately shot her down, declaring "one kid was enough expense for their family." Stephanie pretended not to care about what he said, but the way he'd worded it seemed so insensitive. Naturally that was lost on him.

Stephanie knew Chad "made good money," if only because the joint checking account she used for paying the monthly expenses, wasn't even the one the mortgage was paid out of. She never thought about it, but she didn't even have access to that account, and if something (heaven forbid) ever happened to Chad, she wouldn't know what to do, financially or otherwise. Her name was on the mortgage, along with Chad's, but what good would that do her if she didn't have the money to pay it?

After finishing the housework, Stephanie intended to go through some of the papers Chad kept in a desk drawer in the sunroom, which doubled as his office, overlooking the walled backyard. He usually didn't bring any work home and shouldn't have needed to, given how much of his life he already gave to Quiet Golf Car Company. She wasn't trying to be sneaky, looking for bank account statements when Chad wasn't home. She just figured it was something she could make herself aware of without having to bother her husband. It was possible he would become defensive if she suddenly appeared curious about "their" finances. Then again, maybe she was trying to snoop.

One adjective that definitely did not describe Chad was "free-spirited," and he'd gotten even worse since they'd moved to Arizona. He did make an effort to improve his golf game here, however. Why not, given the fact he could play year-round, and there were many courses from which to choose. So he deserved credit for making at least some effort, but he went through instructor after instructor. Finally one had the nerve to tell him he was better off taking up another hobby. Stephanie always wondered if that guy knew the levity of what he'd told Chad. He ended up pushing his super-expensive clubs into the far corner of the garage, although her parents visited last Thanksgiving and saw them. He should have thrown a towel over them prior to their arrival.

It-Girl and Other Stories

Stephanie's dad asked Chad to play nine holes with him and his wife, but Chad refused. The remainder of her parents' visit, Stephanie's father kept offering to give Chad some pointers. Chad and Stephanie had one of the few houses in Turquoise Estates without a pool in the backyard, so Chad and his father-in-law could have practiced their swings there, side-by-side. Fortunately Stephanie's parents only stayed three days.

Sometime before this weekend, Chad would have to pull the clubs out of the corner and at least swing a few of the clubs a couple times each, no matter how hopeless of a player he was.

Chad couldn't believe the terrible day he had at work. He was counting on Stephanie having made something good for dinner. In the meantime he was stuck in a massive traffic snarl on the 101 Freeway, going nowhere fast. It gave him plenty of time to think, which he didn't like to do, not when it came to his personal life. As much as he loved his wife, it was almost impossible to communicate with her because she was so sensitive. He still maintained she didn't have enough to do, which allowed her "the leisure" to dwell on things. Admittedly, however, she appeared happier overall than when she did have a job. Selfish though it probably sounded, he enjoyed knowing he was the only one comfortably providing for the family. At times he still felt guilty for making them leave Toledo, where Stephanie's parents still lived. Nonetheless, Chad's salary at QGCC almost doubled when he transferred here, so that alone made the move worth it. His family was spread out across the country, and no one even got along with one another, so he didn't have to worry about his own living situation in regard to other family members.

What had ruined Chad's work day was his boss stopped in his (Chad's) office right before lunch and reiterated (yet again) Chad had to play in the company golf tournament

Amy Kristoff

Saturday at Estrella Country Club in Scottsdale. Immediately Chad couldn't help thinking this was perhaps the first "test" in regard to his raise/ promotion. If Chad balked and flat-out refused to play in the tournament, would he not only fail to be promoted but fired? He honestly did not want to find out, so he would be playing in the tournament this weekend. Before then he would be making a trip to the driving range, and he positively dreaded it. Hopefully another "test" didn't consist of him having to score under a hundred for eighteen holes.

Also, Chad was informed (by his boss) he had to take "a guest" to lunch tomorrow at "The Danube." It wasn't the worst fate, and maybe it was another "test," pertaining to a possible raise/ promotion. The lunch tab was already paid, as Mr. Ganin had given Chad three hundred-dollar bills to cover it and could keep the change. The food and service there was excellent, so Chad expected to enjoy himself, even if he was also inadvertently taking a test.

Chad didn't end up breaking any records getting home, but he did make up some time after exiting the freeway. Otherwise he would have called Stephanie to let her know he was going to be late. Maybe he should have called her after all, just to warn her of his arrival, since she jumped when he appeared in the kitchen. She was standing to the left of the sink, peeling carrots. That was her favorite vegetable, and she ate them raw, without even dipping them in dressing. That was the only way Chad and Darlene could eat them.

"I didn't hear you come in," Stephanie told Chad by way of greeting.

Before she could bother to peel another carrot, Chad told her, "Honey, let's go out to dinner."

"Now?" Stephanie asked. Where had Chad's spontaneity been all these years? That was the real question.

"Sure, why not," Chad replied. "Just the two of us."

"What about Darlene, not to mention the roast in the oven?"

It-Girl and Other Stories

"Cut some slices for her and throw the rest in the fridge," Chad said. "While you do that, I'll call Mrs. Zimm to sit for us."

"She's not babysitting anymore," Stephanie said. "She had some health issues, and she moved in with her daughter."

"How about the sitter who has an ad on the mailbox stand?" Chad asked. "I could run down there and get her number." Then he did, not even waiting to make sure that was O.K. with Stephanie! He was as confused as she was about his sense of urgency to take her out to dinner, after looking forward to enjoying something she cooked. Maybe he was stressed from all the sudden weirdness at work. As it was, they hadn't gone out in ages. She went out occasionally for lunch with her friend, Micaela. Being a real estate agent, Micaela went out often.

"Everything will be fine," Chad reassured Stephanie one last time as he drove her to "Old Town Scottsdale." They were going to take a stroll and then pick a restaurant for dinner. Chad had wanted to splurge and take her to "The Danube," but he was afraid he wouldn't be able to keep his mouth shut about having to take an associate of his boss' there tomorrow for lunch. Another part of "the test/ order" was he was forbidden to tell anyone what he was instructed to do. It made Ganin look ridiculous, was probably why. Again, Chad didn't dare question what his boss told him to do, in case Chad's livelihood depended on it.

As it was, Stephanie couldn't seem to make a decision about anything, almost like she was afraid to do so. It was amazing she agreed to let Carla Passel, an eighth-grade neighborhood entrepreneur, babysit Darlene for a couple hours. When Chad had called the number on her flyer at the mailbox stand, she was very eager for the opportunity to be of service and offered to provide some references. Chad didn't think that was necessary, since she lived only four houses to the west, with her divorced mother, who was a nurse. Mrs. Passel often worked the three to eleven shift, so Carla liked to be busy then too.

The second Chad laid eyes on Carla Passel, he couldn't help staring at her, she was so gorgeous. Also, she looked much "older" than an eighth-grader. However, Darlene appeared to take an immediate liking to her, so that should have guaranteed everything would be all right.

While Chad searched for a diagonal parking space near the Fifth Avenue shops, art galleries, and restaurants, Stephanie pointed out her choice, and he obediently parked in it. Truthfully he didn't want to park their new Toyota Camry (identical to the company car) in such a tight space, but Stephanie might start crying if he didn't.

Unfortunately they happened to be parked right in front of "South of the Border," which Chad hated. Naturally Stephanie liked the place, so South of the Border it was. And the walk would take place after dinner, instead. The length of it would depend on how crazy Stephanie got about hurrying back home to Darlene.

Seated in the restaurant, Stephanie wasn't talkative, but she certainly didn't appear to be mad. After a glass of wine, she definitely became more relaxed. The only time she drank was when they went out. He'd pointed out to her countless times, she ought to drink a little at home, to de-stress. She'd look at him like he had three heads.

Overall, the dinner date was a success, at least as far as Chad was concerned. The stroll they took after dinner wasn't as long as he would have liked, however. Stephanie became worried and decided they needed to return home to check on Darlene and the sitter. Stephanie had in fact texted and called Carla, but she hadn't responded.

On the drive home, Chad could hardly believe how much more anxious Stephanie became. She began literally rocking forward, as if trying to make the car go faster. He was in turn compelled to drive faster! Maybe Carla was so busy keeping

It-Girl and Other Stories

Darlene amused she forgot about her phone. (He did not bother telling Stephanie this.)

As Chad turned into the driveway, the Camry's headlights caught some movement on the lighted front stoop, and he acknowledged seeing Darlene. Then he realized that wasn't supposed to be the case! Meanwhile, Stephanie leaped out of the car while it was still moving, and Chad hit the garage door button on the remote, distractedly watching the door ascend. He had his own way of dealing with the situation, and it didn't appear any harm had been done to Darlene, other than she had been locked out of her own house.

Just as Chad exited the garage (via the doorway), he witnessed two people run right past him, headed straight west. One was a tall, lanky "male youth," while his female companion was none other than Carla Passel. Chad was going to be in far more trouble with his wife than Carla would be with her mother.

Chad was going out again Tuesday, this time for lunch in downtown Phoenix, at The Danube. He had his boss' secretary, Tracy Lutz, in the company car as his passenger, as she was "the guest" he was supposed to entertain. Resentment was running high with Chad at the moment, as the excursion made less and less sense. The only good part so far was Tracy had been texting someone ever since she sat down in the car and appeared to have no inclination to make conversation. It was nothing personal, but he had absolutely nothing to say to her, either.

The luncheon would be over soon, Chad kept telling himself while walking ahead of Tracy into the restaurant. It was impossible to imagine why Chad had to bring her here, of all places. They could have gone someplace more casual, cheaper, and closer to QGCC's headquarters. It remained unclear why he was put in this predicament, his speculation about a "test," aside.

Amy Kristoff

During lunch, Chad continued to not have a single thing to talk about with Tracy, other than the possible "why" behind the fact they were seated together at The Danube. He was trying to think of how to bring up the subject. They were at a table for four, and Tracy had insisted upon sitting to Chad's left, versus across from him. She was still texting someone, although not as incessantly as she had been in the car. She found time to gobble up a couple thick, soft sourdough bread sticks, washed down with a glass of white wine. Did she forget it was only lunchtime?

Tracy finally revealed her version of why their boss sent them off to lunch: "I'm not supposed to tell you anything personal because it's part of 'the deal' between Len and me. We have to break up after four years 'cause our relationship's not going anywhere. Hello! He's the married one and refuses to do anything about it. I've been the one inconvenienced all this time and kept waiting. He must hope you need some companionship and can throw me on you."

"I'm married," Chad stated. He put that out there so he didn't have to look like a bad guy for refusing this woman's advances, if it came to that. Tracy definitely appeared to be slightly inebriated (and more uninhibited?). One thing was for sure: she had scooted her chair closer to Chad while she was talking. He became very uneasy.

Lunch arrived, and Tracy ordered another glass of wine. She proceeded to dive into her fettuccini and slurped it like a pig. Chad would have gotten sick merely trying to imitate how she ate. Listening to her was bad enough. Ever since moving to Arizona, he was super-stressed and noises irritated him. He was aware Stephanie thought he was "picking on her" because he hated the sound of the vacuum cleaner, but it really did piss him off to listen to it! Therefore, she made sure not to vacuum when he was home, and how could he not love her for that alone?

Chad was enjoying his steamed haddock with green beans while thinking about Stephanie. The next thing he knew, there was a hand on his upper left thigh. Every time he attempted to (discreetly) get the hand off him, it gripped more tightly. There was nothing romantic about the situation.

As much as Chad wanted to finish his delicious meal, it was impossible, so he stood up to leave, throwing two of the hundred-dollar bills Ganin gave him, on the table. That would easily cover the check and the tip. He told Tracy he'd wait in the car while she finished eating. She proceeded to get up and put her arms out as if to stop him but was too drunk and "missed him." Just as Chad turned to throw his napkin on the table (having started to leave with it), Tracy managed to plant a sloppy kiss on his cheek.

Realtor Micaela Cutler happened to be in The Danube having lunch with two clients of hers, when who traipsed in but her friend Stephanie Havelin's husband, Chad, and his concubine or whatever a drunk slut was supposed to be called when showing her classlessness in public. The couple was sufficiently far away, Chad never had a clue Micaela saw him. That was good because she could tell Stephanie all about what her husband was up to, and it would be impossible for him to defend himself.

Micaela just had to boast about the fact she'd just shown her clients the property that was "The One," so the three of them were here to celebrate before heading back to her office at Arroyo Realty in Scottsdale to write up an offer. Although the million-dollar property would be a second home for the couple, they planned to eventually live there full-time.

Anyway, given the way Chad suddenly upped and left before finishing his meal, he probably got spooked, having never before gone anywhere with the woman (aside from whatever they did in bed). Having realized what a lush she was, he hopefully learned to meet up with her in the sack and nowhere else, certainly not The Danube. Micaela never did think much of Chad, and the feeling was probably mutu-

Amy Kristoff

al.

In the lunch line Tuesday, Darlene heard Mitzi Christensen bragging to anyone who would listen (including Mitzi's latest, best friend, Janet Blake), she was attending a horse show this weekend with her new pony, "Popsicle." He also had a "registered name," but she wasn't sure what it was. Her mom knew, however, because she had the pony's "papers." Darlene wished she could just sit on a pony one time to see what it felt like. So far, whenever she'd asked her mother if she could ride, she was told, "It's too dangerous."

Sometimes Mitzi sat at the same cafeteria table as Darlene, except at the far end. On this particular day Mitzi was sitting at another table but was literally right behind Darlene. Nonetheless, it was difficult to hear what Mitzi had to say because it was so loud. Darlene did pick up something about Mitzi wanting to jump rope after lunch and needed someone to hold the rope besides Janet. Darlene wanted to turn around and volunteer her services but didn't want Mitzi to know she'd been eavesdropping – or trying to. Darlene had a lot of respect for Mitzi, if only because she seemed so much more sure of herself than the other girls (and obviously her family had some money). Therefore, Darlene wanted to try and be her friend. She'd start by offering to hold the jump rope.

Darlene was hungry but could hardly be bothered to eat her meatloaf slice, buttered roll and fruit cup because she anticipated when Mitzi and Janet would be heading to the playground. It was imperative she eat at least some of it, or a cafeteria monitor might call her on it. Worse, she could be forced to spend recess inside because she would be suspected of being sick. She might even be sent to the nurse, who would end up calling Darlene's mother. She (her mother) was still upset about what happened to Darlene the evening before, when the sitter, Carla, purposely locked Darlene out of the house. That had happened after Carla's boyfriend had showed up. Carla had promised it would only be for a few minutes, but it seemed longer. Then Darlene's parents came home from going out to dinner, so it wasn't a big deal. Darlene's mom thought it was, though. She didn't even speak to Darlene's father the whole rest of the evening, nor this morning, that Darlene was aware. She just kept glaring at him.

Darlene thought she was smooth, walking right up to Mitzi and Janet on the playground, offering to hold one end of the jump rope. They looked at each other, both apparently surprised by the offer. Soon, however, the jump rope game was underway.

Tommy Calder had been dribbling a basketball not far from where Darlene Havelin had been talking to Mitzi Christensen and Janet Somebody. Mitzi was stuck-up and her friend Janet was ugly, but Darlene was another matter. It was safe to say he had a crush on her, and he "hated" her for making him feel this way! Hopefully what he was about to do, killed the feeling and kept Mitzi from being interested in him (he knew she was). It was too bad girls were so dumb because most of them sure were pretty!

Tommy proceeded to watch the three commence jumping rope, with Darlene and Janet holding each end, and Mitzi doing the actual jumping. It didn't take long before she was showing off, which made Tommy think she was even more stuck-up than he'd previously concluded. There was only so much he could take before he laid down his basketball and walked right up to Darlene like he was supposed to, giving her a firm push before anyone had a clue what he was up to. Darlene went straight to the pavement, still holding the jump rope, while Janet screamed and dropped her end. She moved out of Mitzi's way as she fell to the ground, her right wrist bending unnaturally.

It didn't appear as if Darlene had been seriously injured, but it was nonetheless decided she was going home early. Her mother had been contacted before Darlene had even left the playground. She dreaded her mother's overreaction, how she treated everything anymore. At least she didn't have to go to the hospital, like Mitzi. Darlene was supposed to accompany her father to the driving range this evening, but she'd probably be forced to stay home. And she'd been looking forward to the excursion because her father spent so little time with her.

Nothing was right for Stephanie Tuesday, from the moment she woke up. She tried to feel better by cleaning the whole house again. By eleven-thirty she was ready for a shower and then a trip to the supermarket. She was out to prove to Chad she could cook something he'd be excited enough about to stay home and eat instead of running out to a restaurant. That way they never had to leave Darlene alone, in the hands of an irresponsible sitter.

As soon as Stephanie returned from grocery shopping, the phone rang. It was Micaela, sounding out of breath as she said, "I had to call you, Stephanie. What I saw at 'The Danube' gave me no choice. And I have two clients waiting for me in the other room, to write up an offer for a property I found them. This is just too important. It's about Chad and his girlfriend."

After Stephanie was told about the escapades of her husband and his lover, she was numb. The description of "the other woman" indicated she might be Chad's boss' secretary, Tracy Lutz. Finally it was no wonder Chad was gunning for a promotion: he'd be getting "her" for his own, personal use!

Stephanie's imagination (and her OCD) went into overdrive following the phone call from Micaela. Over and over (and over) the scene with Chad and Tracy in The Danube, played in Stephanie's head. In the meantime she put the groceries away. Barely had she finished when the phone rang again. It was a representative of Darlene's school. She'd fallen down at recess and needed to be picked up immediately, although she only suffered some minor scrapes. Stephanie couldn't help giggling when she was told that, probably sounding like she'd lost her mind. Perhaps she had.

Dinner couldn't have been more anticlimactic—if that was even the right word. Stephanie had gone to all sorts of trouble to make everything, purchasing ingredients specifically for the meal, and Chad scarfed it down, not paying any attention to what he was putting in his mouth. He wasn't exactly a conversationalist, but he didn't say a single word the whole meal. Stephanie wanted to scream, "Hello! I'm here, Chad! Look at me! Talk to me before it's too late!" She had no idea where the last plea came from, other than deep inside her soul.

Thankfully Darlene provided some momentary encouragement by declaring, "This is really good. I hope you make it again sometime."

Stephanie nodded and Chad said, "As soon as you finish, honey, we'll head over to the driving range."

"Not even a cup of decaf first?" Stephanie asked.

"I'd better not," Chad replied. "I don't want to keep Darlene out too late."

Stephanie looked not only resigned but very depressed. Chad didn't notice, as usual. Besides, he was already getting up from the table and was thinking of what he needed to grab for the driving range. Darlene was scraping her plate clean with her fork and was about to use her right index finger, except her mother would scold her—if she noticed. In this case it was possible she wouldn't even care. There wasn't even any resistance from her in regard to letting Darlene go to the driving range, despite Darlene's fall at the playground and the school nurse telling Darlene's mother her daughter needed to rest the remainder of the day.

The outing at the driving range turned out to be a total disaster. Chad was glad Darlene was too young (and uneducated about golf) to realize the balls Daddy hit were supposed to go airborne when hit from a tee. There wasn't another soul at the driving range, or his cover would have been blown. He wouldn't have hit a whole medium bucket of balls if there had been anyone else around besides his daughter and himself.

Never was Chad so relieved to be done with something, and he hoped to feel similarly relieved tomorrow when he quit his job at Quiet Golf Car Company, eliminating having to play in the company golf tournament. Carl Dante was welcome to be the one chosen to move ahead instead of himself. Chad didn't have what it took to put up with his boss' eccentricities any longer. Fortunately Chad had enough money saved, he could afford to be unemployed for a few months while he sought new employment. If Stephanie ever thought he was secretive about their financial situation, it was only to make sure they had sufficient funds for a time such as this.

In fact, Stephanie always thought Chad didn't communicate with her, but it was difficult for him. However, he intended to communicate loud and clear what his plans were and that in his heart, his family really did come first.

Before Chad had even pulled into the driveway, something didn't seem right. Then he realized the lights for the front stoop weren't on. Unlike the lights on either side of the garage door, they had to be turned on manually. Stephanie always turned them on when she was home. She never went out alone in the evening, not even to walk around the block.

As much as Chad wanted to believe Stephanie had decided to take nap after preparing a five-star meal, he couldn't. Then he stared at the closed garage door, unable to bring himself to press the remote. Instead he dialed 9-1-1 and wondered how she could have done this to Darlene.

Dead Wait

Our dear mother was prone to call me Sheila, when she'd see me out of the corner of her eye. She'd been doing that since forever. It irritated me when I was young, but as time wore on, I realized I could make her lack of observational skills, work in my favor. And Sheila got in trouble for stuff I did!

Sheila was three years older than me, yet she looked younger. I had three divorces to my credit, but I still believed in true love. In fact I was in love with someone – her husband! (Randall was her first husband and her high school sweetheart.) He suspected the crush I'd had on him over the years, and it was time to make good on my desire. I wanted a happily ever after too, and I determined it could only be if he and I were together. Obviously there was an obstacle in the way, in the form of my sister. "The problem" was the fact Randall would never cheat on Sheila. The two really did love one another, and I was happy for them up to a point. Sheila was also extremely obedient. As it was, I didn't want an illicit affair with Randall; I was forty and finished with dead-end relationships. I wanted one last marriage and I wanted it to last. I was certain he and I could "make it work," if only because he got along so well with her yet she was more high-maintenance. We looked a lot alike and our mannerisms were similar, but our personalities were very different. Again, my sister was in the way. I didn't wish her dead; I wished she'd just up and leave, never to return, which sounded even more irrational than killing her.

Amy Kristoff

Our dear mother (her name was Sylvia) deserved all the blame for compelling me to think like this. She made no secret of the fact Sheila was her favorite and why shouldn't she be? Sheila was the first born and her husband was the very successful owner of a landscape design business, catering to the mega-wealthy. The only thing Sheila ever did wrong was never give our dear mother any grandkids, not that there wasn't still time.

Appropriately Sheila and Randall were having a bash to celebrate their twenty-fifth wedding anniversary. It was taking place at their mountainside home that overlooked the Phoenix valley. The view alone was so stunning, you didn't pass up an invitation such as this. (Plus, the landscaping around the house was phenomenal.) As much as I wanted to stay home and sulk because I didn't even have a date to take me, I realized this might just be my golden opportunity to make a move on Randall. I became both excited and apprehensive about the mere prospect. After all, I would be devastated if he rebuffed me. Then again, what did I have to lose? Not knowing what he really thought of me, appeared to be making me go insane. Admittedly, I didn't really know him but did plenty of fantasizing! His mother had him at sixteen and never married Randall's father. When she married someone else later, she kept her maiden name. I didn't even know the last name of her husband, and they had a son, Ryan (Randall's half-brother).

Sheila and Randall planned on an all-nighter, and the booze would be freely flowing, although neither one was a heavy drinker. It was possible there would even be some drugs, as Randall liked cocaine. I intended to get soused, the easier to seduce him. Also, if things didn't pan out between us, I could later blame my behavior on alcohol.

I needed to make a plan, aside from getting drunk. For one, if I showed up early, I couldn't immediately get wasted and throw myself at him. Our dear mother would naturally be one of the attendees, along with our hen-pecked father,

It-Girl and Other Stories

Merrill, a recently-retired financial advisor. He was still pretty spry at seventy, and his wife was too, at sixty-three, but they wouldn't be staying long. As it was, I would stay at the party until enough guests had either left or passed out, and I would make my move. Of course Sheila would have to be one of those in the latter group, although she would probably also be the bartender, hence she would have to stay more sober than everyone else. She enjoyed the responsibility, even if it was her own party. If she wasn't an aesthetician who co-owned "Ella" beauty salon, she probably would have co-owned a bar and would have been one of the bartenders. Even though I accused her of being more high-maintenance than me in a relationship, she was more willing to take on work-related responsibilities and be on her feet a lot. For all the money she and Randall made, they spent it like crazy. Sheila made no secret of wanting to eventually sell her business, once she inherited some "major moolah" (her words) from our dear mother, the wealthier of the two parents.

The party was two days away. Having gone through my closet to find a suitable outfit, I concluded it was time to go shopping. First, however, I put together a bag of clothes I would never wear, to drop off in a donation bin. Coincidentally Sheila and I were about the same size, and although her taste was different from mine, I wondered what it would be like to try on some of her things. Then our dear mother called. She was furious whenever I didn't answer my phone because she knew I had nothing to do all day. The fact I was driving wasn't an excuse, as far as she was concerned. I happened to be nearing a restaurant parking lot, so I pulled in and parked, away from the car and foot traffic.

Our dear mother always started out with the best of intentions when she called me. In her mind, however, I was an ongoing disappointment. Although she was only twenty when she had Sheila and hardly ready to be a mom (our dear mother's assessment), she relished the role. The only reason she had me was so she could experience the whole diaper-changing phase again because she liked it so much. It was frustrating having a child (me) who acted so childish, in middle age! My father used to handle my finances, but my third ex-husband, Greg, was a financial advisor too, so he took over everything. He was the only one of my three exes who remained on speaking terms with me. It just so happened I took the least amount of money from him in the divorce and put yet another advisor in charge of my finances. At least I didn't get involved with him.

After my mother greeted me and asked how I was doing, I replied, "I'm going shopping to find something to wear for Sheila and Randall's party."

"I can't imagine you don't have anything, Starla," she said. "Back when you and Ron lived on Sunburst Circle, you had two walk-in closets to yourself, stuffed with clothes."

"Being married to Ron compelled me to shop for things I didn't need." Ron was my second husband, a photographer, who was wealthy even before he "made it." Between the two of us, we spent money like there was no tomorrow, not unlike Sheila and Randall. It was a fun time of my life, until I found out he was sleeping with many of the models at the photo shoots.

"Sometimes, Starla, I don't understand your line of reasoning."

"Did you call to pick on me yet again?"

"No, I didn't. So. Are you seeing anyone?"

"Believe it or not, no," I replied, hardly able to believe it, myself.

"I don't know how you do it, not working at the very least. Maybe you'd meet a man that way."

"That'll never happen," I told her and wanted to spill my secret about Randall. That would have shut her up because she would have been too shocked to talk anymore. I added, "The only way I'd get a job was if I was bored, which I'm not."

"Fine! I was just trying to be helpful. Oh! I have another call, I think it's Sheila," our dear mother said. "I'll see you at the party." Then she ended the call and that was that. No wonder I couldn't stand our dear mother. She was going to think even less of me before long, and I was actually looking forward to as much! As it was, if anything happened to her, everything was probably going to Sheila, although Sheila thought the opposite was the case – and was obsessed with that possibility.

    The clothing donation bin in which I'd intended to drop off the clothes, was no longer in the parking lot of "Peabody's," a supermarket at the corner of Hayden Road and Shea Boulevard. On the way to the mall, via Shea Boulevard, there was a non-denominational church that had a resale shop. Even if it wasn't open, there was most likely a drop-off bin available.

    Reaching the parking lot of the church, right away I noticed a banner above the entryway for the resale shop. On it, the hours were posted: Monday, Wednesday, and Friday, 11-3. There was also a bin to the right of the glass door leading to the resale shop. In the parking lot there were a number of vehicles, including a shabby-looking, white pickup truck with "Mark Murzo Landscaping and Maintenance" on the side. It wasn't a last name you saw every day, and I happened to have gone to sixth through eighth grades with a boy who had that first and last name. I liked him because he was friendly and polite, versus mean-spirited, how many of the other boys were.

    Since I wasn't much for social media, I didn't keep up with former classmates' doings, unless it was someone I had been close to for several years. Supposedly Mark's younger brother had a rare neurological disorder that could only be treated at a hospital in Boston. The whole family left Arizona to live close to the medical facility. The climate here must have helped induce Mark to return to the area and have his own business. If I needed any yard work done, it was understood I would only use my brother-in-law's company, so I never needed to look around for a landscaping or yard care service. Currently I was living in a condo that barely had a yard, and it was maintained through the homeowner's association. Even when Randall's company took care of yard maintenance, I'd rarely see him, as his crew would show up to do the work.

A sign on the resale shop's door read: "If you are here during business hours, please bring items inside. Thank you." I was about to open the door when who had to be Mark was exiting. He ended up holding the door open for me, obviously to be polite, not because he recognized me. I wanted to say, "Mark?" but couldn't because I was tongue-tied! He had a couple shirts draped over is right arm, and he just kept going. By the time I glanced behind me, he seemed to have disappeared. I couldn't believe how good he looked.

I decided the best thing to do was look up his landscaping business online when I got home. Through that I could contact him and apologize for not saying hello. He was forgiven if he didn't recognize me, as I looked better than ever (if I did say so, myself) and didn't even resemble the chubby-faced girl I once was.

The mall suddenly didn't seem like such an enticing place to shop, so I ended driving back toward home. Then I decided I needed a manicure, and I happened to be passing "The Gold Buckle" strip mall, at the corner of Shea and Goldwater, where the nail salon I frequented was located. The array of businesses included a vintage clothing shop, not far from "Nails By Kate & Co." If Kate couldn't give me a manicure on short notice, I'd look for an outfit at "Treasure Trove," as I was suddenly inspired to be thrifty, regarding it as a challenge to find something tasteful yet alluring to wear.

I wanted to be early to the party to enjoy the sunset on the patio of Sheila and Randall's. Also, I wanted to see our dear mother and father. You'd think given the way she treated me, I'd be compelled to avoid her, but the opposite was the

It-Girl and Other Stories

case. Besides, I wanted her to see how terrific I looked, including the fire engine red nails. Kate talked me into the color, as I'd told her I was doing something daring at the party, not elaborating. However, I did describe the ensemble I'd purchased at Treasure Trove: white lace shirt with a plunging neckline; a black velour corset fringed with colorful beads; and a black nylon skirt that went halfway down my calves with slits most of the way up my thighs. The look was slutty female matador? Something like that. At least no one else would be dressed like me, although Sheila might outdo me when it came to being "daring."

After I parked my white Alfa Romeo in front of the three-car garage, leaving plenty of room for the other guests to park behind me as well around the fountain in the middle of the circular, tan brick driveway, Sheila bounced out the front doorway to greet me, wearing a sheer, pale pink, long-sleeved blouse with a high collar. It sounded prim, but you could see right through the fabric and she wasn't wearing a bra. And her long blond hair was in a loose bun atop her head, so none of it was draped around her shoulders, covering anything. At least her white pants weren't see-through too. She gave me a quick hug and thanked me for coming. She could be so nice to me, usually right before doing something dastardly. Well, it worked both ways.

"Love your outfit," she said. "What have you been up to? Where's your date?"

"Who would that be? I'm not seeing anybody."

"You? Come on! Hey, I saw your ex Ron the other day."

"Ugh. Where was he?"

"Leaving Peabody's with one of his hot young things he never seems to tire of."

"He's trying to hold onto his youth."

"It doesn't look like whatever he's doing is working, if it makes you feel any better."

"Did he at least say hello?"

"He didn't even notice me. I'm too old for him and I wasn't

dressed like this!"

"I thought I ran into Mark Murzo from sixth grade through eighth grades, a couple days ago. It sure looked like an adult version of him. He had or has a landscaping business, so I tried to look him up that evening . . . nothing. Maybe somebody bought his old truck and that guy wasn't even him."

"Well, come in the house and have a drink. Ask Randall about him, he might know."

I followed Sheila in the house, via the front door, which was ajar. To the left of the foyer there were double French doors, leading to a spacious sitting area that had a bar in the far right corner. There was oak wood flooring throughout the house, aside from the kitchen and foyer, which had tan slate. Beyond the floor-to-ceiling windows on the east side of the sitting room was the lap pool. It was in fact perpendicular to the flagstone patio, where I liked to sit and enjoy the view. The layout of the property was dictated by the huge rock formations that were on either side, which provided even more privacy. Nonetheless the pool area was enclosed by a tall, black wrought-iron fence. Various plant and flower species grew seemingly everywhere, and the house even had flower boxes in the upstairs windows. The house in fact looked like an English cottage (except it was close to six-thousand square feet).

Sheila went behind the bar and I stood close by but was looking out at the pool. She said, "Randall just finished a swim a few minutes ago and went up to take a shower. . . So, what'll you have?"

"Sparkling wine would be good," I replied.

"That's what I'll have, I think," Sheila said and set out two champagne flutes before opening a bottle of Cristal.

"Wow! Glad you're splurging!"

"Randall bought several bottles. We're celebrating, remember? He even almost got his mother and stepdad to fly in from Seattle. Ryan will probably stop by, though"

It-Girl and Other Stories

(Randall's half-brother).

"Happy Anniversary!" I said and then started to look away until noticing my sister was furtively emptying some powder into the champagne flute closest to me.

"Starla! Welcome!" Randall exclaimed as he appeared from the kitchen, the doorway leading to it to the right of the bar. I caught a quick look at Sheila's face and she appeared ready to scream in anger. Had she been about to drug me and possibly kill me? In my family anything was possible, and I was as guilty as any of them to go to extremes.

Randall and I embraced. After he complimented me on how "lovely" I looked, he told Sheila, "Babe, go get us some coke. I want to do some before your parents arrive, in case they decide to stick around and I get a craving."

"Bill and Sandy will be bringing some," Sheila said. "Theirs is always worth waiting for, even if we have to wait for our parents to leave."

"Sheila honey, please go get the coke, O.K.?" Randall told her, and she left the room in a huff. One thing she never failed to be was the obedient wife. I could never outdo her on that one, no matter how much I might love someone.

Meanwhile, I wondered if I really knew which glass had the powder in it. I'd say it was a sexual enhancement drug for Randall, except she'd poured the two drinks for us. I didn't know what to do, other than not have any champagne, after all. I'd tell her I wasn't feeling well. Meanwhile, I sat on one of the metal-backed bar stools, which had a plush, off-white Naugahyde cushion.

Then Randall reached for one of the glasses, saying, "Coke goes great with this," and handed me the glass I was certain contained the suspicious powder. I wondered if I should tell him what I saw. Would he believe me?

Sheila reappeared with a small plastic bag of cocaine, a portion of a plastic straw, and a black credit card. She went behind the bar and set everything down in front of Randall, who couldn't wait to lay out some lines, as the top of the bar

79

had glass on it. He didn't need to chop it up, so he proceeded to eagerly snort a huge line. Afterward he looked in the direction of the front door and asked, "Did some more guests just drive up? Sheila, make sure it isn't your parents." Then he handed me the straw and told me to do a line. Fortunately the two that remained were much smaller than the one he just did. I'd barely eaten anything all day, so I hoped this didn't make me sick. I hadn't done enough drugs in my life to know which ones were the most hellish if your body wasn't up to the abuse. All I knew was I did not want to drink the glass of champagne with the powder in it. Snorting cocaine somehow seemed "safer."

Sheila temporarily disappeared but not before looking closely at the champagne flutes. Randall was oblivious to her interest in them and said, "The only problem with coke is it makes me so damn horny! But that's where the bubbly comes in, tempers everything." Then he reached for the same glass he'd originally given me and I thought was tainted.

"Shouldn't you get the cocaine off the bar in case our parents really are the ones who just showed up?" I asked, buying some time before he drank out of "the glass."

"Yeah, I guess so," he said and proceeded to snort the line intended for Sheila. Afterward he stuck the straw and credit card in his front left pocket, which was small, typical of the style of jeans he was wearing. "God, do I feel good now. I'd gone swimming because I felt stiff and sore all over, but the coke took care of everything!"

Sheila appeared and behind her was our dear mother, saying, "I thought you were greeting me, Starla, not Sheila, when I saw her risqué top." Then our dear mother headed straight for the bar. She didn't always drink, so no one ever asked her if she wanted anything. Somehow it offended her. However, she did like champagne on occasion, which Sheila should have kept in mind.

I remarked, "Oh, come on, you know damned well she's always been the one to dress like that, way before me."

It-Girl and Other Stories

"How have you been, honey?" my father asked and I stood to hug him. He got a pretty good look at the slits on my skirt and smiled. He'd thought only Sheila was worth ogling! I was high as a kite on cocaine and didn't have a care in the world. It was better than being drunk.

Randall shook hands with his father-in-law and asked him if he wanted a drink.

"I'll have a scotch on the rocks," Dad replied. Observing Sheila mix the drink, he added, "You sure are quick, just like Randall can landscape a yard. You two ever do anything slow?"

Sheila turned about all the way around to make eye contact with her husband and smiled. They appeared to be so in love it was sickening! Attempting to seduce him seemed more and more like a waste of time. Randall already had a couple opportunities to make a pass at me and nothing happened. However, I could hardly keep my hands off him, especially tonight. Maybe he simply wasn't interested. It proved I could exercise restraint, but I didn't intend to hold back much longer.

Only when Sheila handed Dad his drink did I finally notice both champagne flutes were empty! She looked surprised too but didn't realize I'd noticed. I only had a second to contemplate as much before there was the sound of tires squealing in front of the house. Then a car horn blared.

"That's Ryan," Randall said, heading for the front door. "His way of wishing us 'Happy Anniversary.' He probably won't end up staying."

I decided it was time to go sit on the patio; there was too much commotion already, and one reason I came to the party was to enjoy the view – even alone, on my sister and brother-in-law's 25th anniversary. It wasn't like I cared about mingling with everyone or saying hello to Randall's half-brother, who was so much younger than Randall, he could have been his son. Ryan detailed cars for a living and sold drugs to make extra cash. Most likely he had an anniversary gift for

Amy Kristoff

his older brother: cocaine! Randall couldn't be satisfied with his stash, not to mention what Bill and Sandy would be bringing. Sheila would never admit it, but she wasn't keen on Randall liking cocaine as much as he did. It didn't help with their money problems.

The sun was just setting and there was a slight breeze, with various floral scents filling the late March air. The high from the cocaine was abating, and I wanted some more. However, I preferred to be alone, at least for a few minutes. I had no idea how many guests Sheila and Randall had invited, but they would all most likely show up.

I stood close to the edge of the patio, a mere three feet of stacked limestone between me and a steep drop-off. Just as I was going to turn and sit on a black wrought-iron bench, I felt a hand on each of my elbows. I tried to decipher if I smelled aftershave and if so, what kind it was. I waited a few seconds before slowly turning around and – no one was there! Did the cocaine do this to me or had someone just tricked me? The latter seemed impossible, as there was no place for an individual to hide. Then again, I'd come out here via the kitchen, where there was a large glass door I'd left open. Sheila and Randall were both too busy to have any pets, so there was no chance of a cat or dog slipping outside. I'd wanted to hear the guests arrive so I wasn't totally unaware of the goings on. Maybe it was in fact possible someone could have briefly touched my elbows and then dashed back in the house – but why? Then again, why not? It was a party and everyone was supposed to be having fun.

It suddenly occurred to me who might have drunk the champagne flute with the suspicious powder. As if to confirm as much, I heard Sheila scream, "Mom, no! Quick, Randall, grab her, she's falling!"

Randall must not have gotten to our dear mother in time because I heard a thud. Or maybe he purposely didn't make it in time to save her, as she hit her head pretty good on the bar, before going down. Dad would have been too surprised to help, as well as anyone else standing around her.

Before the ambulance had arrived, Sheila completely unraveled and confessed the following: "I never meant to kill her! It was for Starla!"

Randall had to have been behind Sheila's scheme as well, but she was such an obedient wife, she was taking the fall for him. I did not immediately conclude as much and spent the night with him, once Sheila was carted off to jail and he was effortlessly seduced.

Super-early this morning, Randall left the house, as his crew is landscaping a five-acre estate in nearby Paradise Valley. It's supposed to be hellishly hot today, typical for mid-August. I woke up briefly and fell back to sleep, since I have nothing to do all day. I will when he gets home later in the afternoon, however.

End of the Road

Ronnie Gill lived with his dad, who worked a lot. Ronnie had an active imagination, so he was good at keeping himself amused. Ron elder was grateful for as much, but he sometimes worried whether his son might be lonely. One activity Ronnie enjoyed was riding his bicycle around Woodridge Subdivision, where the two lived, in Round Lake, Indiana. All the houses were new and impressive-looking but had rather small yards. When Ronnie turned eleven he was allowed to cross north-south Morse Street via West 142nd Avenue and follow it until it dead-ended. All the houses on this side were built in the 1920s and 1930s, on spacious lots. The only one that didn't look ramshackle was the one at the very end of the street. It was owned by Ed Dart. In the winter it was possible to see the lake Round Lake was named for, in the distance. If his lot was on the water a developer would have bought it by this time.

Ed was respected simply for taking such excellent care of his house and one-acre property. His house faced West 142nd, so Ronnie could see it long before reaching it. One of Ronnie's favorite activities was guessing what Mr. Dart would be doing when Ronnie approached on his bicycle. In the warmer months, it wasn't unusual to see the old man in a rocking chair, always the one on the left side of the porch. Ronnie wondered if the other rocking chair was the man's wife's, as she had passed away a decade ago.

Because of the amount of shade provided by the oak and hickory trees on Ed Dart's property, there was a minimum of grass-cutting, even in early spring. Ronnie always thought the old man would be grateful for as much, but maybe he liked to cut the grass. Given how well Mr. Dart took care of everything else in regard to his house, that was most likely the case.

Despite the fact Mr. Dart obviously very capably took care of his house and property on his own, one day Ronnie was compelled to stop riding his bicycle long enough to walk to the edge of the porch of Mr. Dart's and ask him if he needed a hand with anything. The old man was sitting in the rocking chair he usually did, but he wasn't moving. Ronnie thought maybe he was tired, having possibly just finished an exerting task. Ronnie liked to think he was pretty good at quite a few odd jobs, as he was expected to help his dad inside and outside their house. Ron (Ronnie's father) had let his son know early on (about the same time Ronnie's mother left, when Ronnie was six), it was going to be just the two of them, so it was imperative Ronnie pull his own weight. Ron the elder had said as much to help make his son feel important, since his mother basically upped and walked away, choosing to move to Chicago and cater to her career in banking, wanting no part of "having it all," not when it came to having her family in the picture.

Intrinsically Ronnie was a very serious-minded kid. Even when playing, he had a sense of duty about whatever he was doing. Therefore, it wasn't too surprising he found it necessary to stop and offer his help to Mr. Dart. As it was, Ronnie had never met the man but had turned his bicycle around in front of the man's house countless times already, despite having been only lately allowed to ride further than the confines of Woodridge Subdivision. His father didn't even have to be home when Ronnie rode his bicycle. He in fact often wasn't, even on Saturday mornings like this one. Ron worked all week as a mechanic at "Pettigrew Automotive Repair," in Round Lake, only a few miles from home. On Saturdays he often helped friends with at-home vehicle repairs, to earn some extra cash. Although his ex-wife, Laura, had to help support their son financially, she wasn't obligated to do much else. She was the one who'd wanted to build a house in Woodridge, as it was the most upscale subdivision in Round Lake. Laura didn't end up being the same woman Ron married, all thanks to her highfaluting banking job. Meanwhile, Ron couldn't yet sell the house because he still owed more on it than it was worth.

"Sir, you need help with anything?" Ronnie asked Mr. Dart.

"No, son, I don't believe I do, but thanks for asking. I've seen you come by here quite a lot. If you don't mind me asking, what is your name?"

"Ronnie Gill, sir."

"You related to a Ron Gill?"

"That's my dad."

"Well I know his boss Jerry, he's an old family friend. He's not as old as me, but we go way back. Your dad changed the windshield wipers on a car for me once. I was having the darnedest time. I used to do all the repair work on the wife's and my cars. Finally bought one brand-new after she passed, so I started going to the dealership and been going there ever since."

"My dad knows your name, sir, because of Jerry Pettigrew, his boss."

"They talking about me behind my back?" Mr. Dart jokingly asked.

Ever serious, Ronnie replied, "Oh no, sir, nothing like that. My dad had mentioned something about your house once, how nice you keep everything. He asked Mr. Pettigrew who lived here because he knows everybody."

"He sure does!" Mr. Dart said and laughed. "So where do you live?"

"Woodridge. Eight-six-three-seven Talon Drive."

"Very good. Thanks again for offering your help. I'll certainly keep you in mind if I need a hand with anything."

It-Girl and Other Stories

Ronnie waved to Mr. Dart and rode away. He was thrilled the old man would even consider putting him to work, even if it was a minor task. He considered circling back and asking Mr. Dart if he would like his phone number (the house land line was all Ronnie had access to), but he didn't want to bother him again.

Ray Dart was soon going to pay his father, Ed, a visit. The two hadn't spoken in several years, and the last phone call consisted of Ed calling his only child a piece of s—t and hanging up on him. Ray had just gotten out of jail, having beaten up his wife one too many times and finally the bitch pressed charges. Ray had been trying to patch things up with her, and she thanked him by slamming him with divorce papers. Rent was overdue on the dump they were living in, so leaving seemed like the best answer, for the time being. To say Ray needed to cool off was putting it lightly. He would deal with her later. He had some catching up to do with his old man, and they were going to do that catching up, whether Pops liked it or not. Ray didn't care if he had to hold a goddamned knife to the old coot's throat to make him sit and talk. The guy was eighty-eight and did more than people half his age – including his son. Actually Ray was fifty-eight, and that was another thing: he'd taken early retirement from the manufacturing plant he'd given over thirty years of the best part of his life to, and they claimed that because of "corporate restructuring," his pension would only be half of what he'd been promised. So much for kicking back and drinking all day. At least he wasn't hard to please. However, he was super-mad, obviously for more than one reason! His father had better hear him out; the old man didn't have a choice.

Ed ended up dozing off in his rocking chair on the front porch of his house, after talking to the Gill kid. Ed had felt exhausted from having washed all the windows, both inside and outside. He'd intended to do the chore in two parts, but

Amy Kristoff

it was such a nice day, he'd decided to do the whole thing. At his age, it simply wasn't as easy as it used to be to take care of his house. Maybe he would ask the Gill boy for some help, the next time he rode his bicycle over here.

Having awakened from his cat nap, Ed continued to keep his eyes closed, but he suddenly had the creepy feeling someone was watching him. He opened his eyes and looked straight ahead, expecting to see the Gill kid. He wasn't anywhere. Ed turned his head to his left and about fell out of his rocking chair upon seeing his estranged son, Ray, staring at him, with a "mirthful" expression, seated in what was formerly his mother's rocking chair. His expression belied what he was really thinking: he wanted to kill his father. Never before had Ed so wished for something: to have Ronnie Gill return and again ask if he could help Ed!

Ed was aware he had very little time to think of a plan. Trying to talk his son out of a demonic act was fruitless. The only two houses pretty close to Ed's were set rather far off the street, like his. They both had overgrown, unkempt shrubs around them and were dwarfed by towering oak trees with thick, leafy, low-hanging branches. The neighbors were older like himself, if not infirm. Should his son decide to drag him into the house to murder him, no one would see Ed put up a fight, and they probably wouldn't hear him scream. Besides, the ruckus would only piss off Ray even more. It would take but a couple seconds for Ray to slit his throat, as he undoubtedly had a knife on him to do the deed. Ray never was one to think about repercussions, and he was getting even more impulsive with age.

After Ronnie returned from Mr. Dart's, he couldn't seem to find anything he wanted to do. He'd already cleaned his room and changed the sheets on his bed, the latter an every Saturday morning chore. The other sheets were finishing drying in the dryer, so he made a bologna sandwich and ate that while waiting. His dad wouldn't be home until 2:30, and he would be grilling some burgers. That seemed like a long ways away. Ronnie couldn't wait until his dad started letting him tag along when he went to people's houses to fix their vehicles. He kept saying Ronnie could accompany him, going on a year or more.

Ronnie went back outside and piddled around the yard for a few minutes before deciding to take another bike ride. He'd probably go back to where Mr. Dart lived – not to pester him about helping, just for a place to ride. A couple doors down, Jeremy Rich was popping wheelies in the driveway, so Ronnie asked him if he wanted to come along on a ride.

"Where to?" Jeremy wanted to know.

"Around here and then down a hundred and forty-second, across Morse," Ronnie replied. "It won't be too much for your little trick bike."

"My bike'll make it. . . I just don't want to go there. A weird old guy lives at the end."

"Mr. Dart?"

"You know him?"

"Kinda. Do you?"

"No, and I don't wanna know him. I heard he's a weirdo."

"Who told you that?"

Jeremy shrugged.

"You're full of shit," Ronnie said. His dad used that word under his breath all the time. Ronnie wasn't supposed to hear him. Ronnie felt like it was imperative to defend Mr. Dart; it made more sense than agreeing with an assumption that came out of Jeremy Rich's mouth.

"See you later," Jeremy said, proceeding to drop his bike in the grass next to the driveway and then going in the house via the opened garage doorway.

Ronnie merely nodded at Jeremy, feeling like he'd already made his point. Then off he went, in the direction of Mr. Dart's. Ronnie was not trying to spy on the old man or become a nuisance; he simply liked where Mr. Dart's house was located. Where Ronnie lived seemed so impersonal; the whole street where Mr. Dart's house was had character, even the houses in disrepair.

Near Mr. Dart's Ronnie discerned a small gray car, which appeared to be a Toyota of some kind, parked in the very middle of the blacktopped driveway, making it impossible to back a vehicle out of the two-car garage.

Unable to resist being nosy, Ronnie stopped his bicycle and got off, walking it up to the car so he could read the license plate, which was from Michigan. Just as he turned his bike around and was about to ride it back down the driveway, the front door was opened. A short, burly-looking older guy with a graying buzz cut and goatee emerged from it, and he couldn't seem to wait to ask Ronnie, "What you lookin' at, sonny boy?" Leaving the door wide open, he proceeded to approach Ronnie, who surprised himself by not feeling any fear (or very little). What riled him up was the "sonny boy" connotation, which was even more prize worthy than Jeremy Rich declaring Mr. Dart was a weirdo.

Something didn't feel right about the whole situation, so Ronnie took the liberty of lying to this guy: "I'm looking for my little dog. He ran away from home and I thought I saw him hiding under that car."

"That's my car, sonny, and dogs don't hide under cars," the meanie replied. "It probably went back home while you're wastin' time lookin' for it." Then he spun around and headed back toward the opened front doorway.

Ronnie couldn't help but linger an extra couple seconds, attempting to process what was bothering him. Obviously the guy was a relative or family friend, and he was visiting Mr. Dart. The last thing Ronnie rode his bike down here to do was meddle, but he felt like it was indeed what he was doing! Then he heard a moan emitted from within the house, right before the meanie slammed the door. Panic rising in him, Ronnie decided the logical course of action was to ride his bicycle home and call for help. He pedaled like a maniac, thanks to his apprehension about Mr. Dart's welfare.

It-Girl and Other Stories

Possibly it was in fact too late for the old man, but Ronnie refused to believe as much.

Ray didn't like to have to torture someone to make his point, not even his old man. He'd started out trying to be reasonable, but his senile father refused to listen. Ray had tried to tell him he'd help keep the house up if he'd just let Ray stay for a few months while he got a job and got on his feet. (Ray decided to pretend his wife wasn't trying to divorce him.) The old geezer had the balls ask, "A job doin' what?" to which Ray responded by grabbing him by the collar of his blue work shirt, ripping it. Then Ray dragged him into the house—the house that had better be his soon. Ray wanted to off the guy but couldn't afford to until he was 100% sure Pops hadn't cut him out of his will. It was even possible there was no will at all, which wasn't the worst thing because Ray was next of kin. Still, Ray wanted to be SURE.

Having sat the coot down in the house, Ray tried to get an answer out of him, whether he had a will and where a copy of it was located. Finally Ray got him to say there was a copy of the will in a safety deposit box at the bank (not giving an exact name), but no one was allowed to look at anything on Saturdays. Ray got so pissed by that pathetic lie, he started beating up his father, getting more and more angry while doing so. The old coot didn't even attempt to defend himself! Then Ray happened to notice something glistening outside and laid off the old man for a minute to investigate what was going on, leaving the front door wide open, daring his father to escape.

It turned out there was a kid, nosing around the property, specifically by Ray's car. Ray became so incensed by the twit's mere presence, he almost tore into him too. Supposedly the kid was looking for his lost dog, some bullshit. He was probably hoping the car doors were unlocked so he could steal something. That was how Ray was at that kid's age. There was nothing Ray's father could have done to make

Amy Kristoff

his son a better person; it simply wasn't in him!

Anyway, the kid left lickety-split, looking pretty scared, which Ray found hilarious. He in fact went back in what was soon going to be his house, wearing a shit-eating grin. Right as he was shutting the door he felt something piercing his back. He started to reach behind him but was pushed against the door and his head was slammed into it at the same time the knife impaled him.

All in the Family

It went without saying, Monica Treble was obsessed with horses because she didn't have a choice. In other words, her mother, Melinda, started out dragging her twelve-year-old daughter to Pinetop Stable on Saturdays, so Mom could have a lesson and not be worried about leaving her daughter home alone. (Melinda feared her daughter might become promiscuous if she didn't keep an eye on her.) Given nothing to do but help around the stable while her mother rode, Monica eventually came to realize she liked horses and wanted to try riding them, too. The resident hunter-jumper trainer, Liam Muir, told her he didn't have anything "slow or small enough" for Monica to learn on. He sent kids like her to his ex-girlfriend's stable, "Waverly Riding Academy," which was actually on the same property as the stable he worked at but in a different barn. Monica was repeatedly told at school she was tall for her age, so she had decided the guy simply didn't like the looks of her. However, his face lit up every time he saw Monica's mom. Her mom was pretty pathetic, herself. Monica often wondered, since her father paid for his wife's lessons (Monica's mother's) was he aware she flirted with her trainer?

By the end of the school year, Monica was interested in horses to the point she wanted to work at a stable part-time, provided her mother could drop her off two or three mornings a week and then pick her up. Maybe she could have a lesson in exchange for helping (but obviously not from Mr. Muir)? Since her mother already had the one day devoted to riding, it didn't seem like it would be too much to ask, to have her take Monica to a stable, one or two other days. Since the property where Pinetop Stable and Waverly Riding Academy were located also had a couple other stables, Monica planned on asking around, to see who would let a twelve-year-old girl work for them. She wasn't planning on it being Liam Muir's, as he couldn't seem to stand having her around even one morning a week, working for free. (Monica dusted the stall fronts, raked the sand aisle way, etc.) Since this was Phoenix, Arizona, barn maintenance was easy. The forty-stall barns on the property didn't even have doors at either end! That explained how one day Monica "caught" Mr. Muir and her mother hugging, just inside the doorway, following her mother's lesson. Monica was so confused! She decided the best thing to do was not say anything for the time being.

"I'd better start riding," Liam said, backing away from Monica's mother. "I've got six to work and then more lessons later."

"Thanks as always for the lesson, Liam," Melinda told him, appearing agitated. She wouldn't even look at her daughter.

"You bet. See you next week," Liam said.

As usual Monica was ignored, which was fine with her. However, she was getting so accustomed to piddling around the barn she didn't want to leave. She wished she was old enough to drive herself to a stable – one where she would be appreciated. Maybe her father needed to be told after all, how much Monica's mother liked her current trainer. It could only work in Monica's favor, right?

This was more like it. Monica was now driven to a totally different stable from Liam Muir's. It wasn't even on the same property. It was on the way to her father's place of business, a flooring company. With school out, Monica could go to the stable seven mornings a week if she wanted but for now she was keeping it at three. Her father picked her up at lunch time and brought her back home. Meanwhile, Monica's mother was basically on house arrest ever since Monica blabbed about what had been going on with the trainer. Initially Monica felt kind of bad about tattling on her, but she concluded her mother deserved the punishment. Strangely, her mother seemed to think she was found out by someone else. Monica was actually disappointed but didn't bother setting the record straight. All she wanted was to drive herself everywhere and not rely on her parents.

What was unsettling about Monica's father, upon finding out what his wife did, was he didn't press Monica for any details. It was like if he knew too much he'd only become angrier. She had a feeling he was biding his time until his only child (herself) turned eighteen, and he was going to divorce Monica's mother. More and more Monica felt like a burden to both parents. She wished she could grow up faster because she felt more mature than her age – and looked it as well, not only because she was tall.

"Chaparral Jumpers, LLC" was the name of the stable Monica had been driven to for close to a month, already. She'd gone online and looked up stables in the area, and on the website for Chaparral Jumpers, LLC, there was an opening for a "working student." She could make her own hours and riding was "optional." The trainer, Terrence Stall (that really was his last name), was very nice to Monica – but not like her mother's former trainer was (to her mother). The unsettling part was Monica had a crush on Terrence. She wanted to think it was a father-daughter kind of feeling, but she couldn't deny she felt something else. Spending time at the new stable was far too important to mention a word to anyone about this, so she kept it to herself. Terrence was a very talented rider, so she liked watching him train the horses, which were all imported from Europe. Her mother's trainer, Liam Muir, wasn't as good and was prone to become impatient with a horse. All the ones he worked with were from the United States, as far as she knew. She never saw him beat one up, but she had seen long spurs with dried blood on them in the tack room back at Pinetop Stable. Monica had asked her mother whose spurs those were one day, and she'd said, "Some cowboy's who comes by every once in awhile and helps Liam get the roguish horses in line. He would never abuse an animal."

Monica wasn't convinced. If Liam Muir had the nerve to hug (or more) a married woman, anything was possible. Monica's mother might have been lucky without realizing it. If both men had decided to "lose it," she could have been trapped in the middle. Was she aware of as much? Her mother always did seem to be pretty clueless, overall. She was definitely selfish.

"How old did you say you were, again?" Terrence asked Monica this morning, shortly after her father had dropped her off. (She was on a Tuesday, Wednesday, Friday schedule.) It was going to be especially hot today, and since Monica wore jeans to the stable no matter the weather, it was imperative she not overdress on top. She didn't think twice about wearing the top half of her red bikini under a short-sleeved white blouse, tucked in but left unbuttoned for the most part. Her mother evidently didn't see what her daughter was wearing before leaving the house this morning, and her father was oblivious to most everything.

Monica just wanted to start working, be it brushing a horse or doing some barn work. The last thing she needed was to be asked a question that had already been posed. The first time around she'd replied, "Fifteen and three-quarters." She'd liked that answer because if it was true, turning sixteen was only three months away. Should Terrence be worried about her working for him (for free) as a minor, it sounded better than the truth. When he appeared about to put his hands on her chest, she quickly said, "I'm not almost sixteen like I told you when you interviewed me."

"Oh?" he said, looking hopeful.

It-Girl and Other Stories

Realizing he most likely expected her to tell him she was in fact eighteen, she did just that! She must have done so in order to see his reaction – which was amazing. However, the luster of that soon wore off, as she became aware of the fact he now considered her completely legal, for all intents and purposes. Already she was in over her head.

One thing Monica did not want to do was get Terrence in any kind of trouble. He seemed like a decent person, but then again she didn't really know him. Truthfully that was how she wanted to keep it. She had enough going on in her personal life, with her parents barely speaking to each other, making a very uncomfortable situation at home. All she had to do was set the record straight – but she couldn't get any words to come out of her mouth. Then it became impossible because Terrence kissed her.

This wasn't the kind of twenty-stall stable where a boarder might suddenly appear and "save her." It was on Terrence's own two-acre property, behind his house. His livelihood consisted of training young jumping horses to be sold to other trainers or their customers, who only showed up if there was an appointment. No one was going to catch him making out with his underage working student, other than perhaps Diego, his groom, the only paid employee Monica was aware of. Most likely Diego made himself scarce if he saw anything outrageous. Even though he didn't reside on the property, he was seemingly always around. Since Terrence wanted the stalls cleaned several times a day, Diego stayed busy with that chore alone.

It was up to Monica if she wanted to be "saved," at this point. It came down to how determined she was to resist a man's advances, despite thinking she had a crush on one. She felt "old enough" for Terrence, despite having zero sexual experience.

With that, Monica attempted to return Terrence's kiss, which made him more aggressive, as he proceeded to place his hands right on top of her breasts, which she found very unnerving. Nonetheless, she pretended to approve by leaning toward him and closing her eyes, hoping that would help her relax. However, she was suddenly self-conscious and wished she'd never let things go this far. She told herself it was what she deserved for lying about her age – twice, no less. The make-out session continued, with Terrence embracing her and putting his face between her breasts. Meanwhile, Monica had slowly started backing up, hoping he would take the hint and not follow her. Unbeknownst to her, she was headed right where he wanted her to: the doorway leading to the air-conditioned tack room. The comfortable, black leather sofa in there was going to be perfect for doing some things. In fact, Allen Snede was bringing a rich amateur customer to ride a couple of recent imports in a little over an hour, so Terrence would stay busy with the girl until then. In truth he didn't give a damn about her age, whatever it was; having been hired as a working student, she should have known something like this was bound to happen. Fortunately he hadn't changed into boots and breeches yet and was still wearing his khakis.

    Joe wanted to think he was a decent husband and father, who provided well for his family. Evidently, however, that wasn't enough, given his wife Melinda's behavior. What was it about trainers? No matter what they were teaching, they spelled trouble for marriages. Joe had yet to confront the horse trainer/riding instructor his wife was into, but he sure as hell put a stop to her weekly riding lessons with the guy. She was undoubtedly communicating with him on her phone, but that would be terminated soon, as well. Joe just needed to figure out how to pry it out of her hands without having to kill her. Either that or he needed to figure out where she kept it hidden, the rare occasion she wasn't playing with it.

    Truthfully, ever since their daughter, Monica, spilled the beans on what her mother was doing with her trainer, Joe had been seeing red. He wanted to tell Melinda to go ahead and leave him for the trainer, but he feared she actually would! The last thing Joe wanted was to finish raising their kid, alone. The second Monica turned eighteen, Joe was done with his marriage. He couldn't wait to be "done" with his daughter, too. It sounded callous, but having a kid had been Melinda's idea. See? There was no pleasing her.

The riding lessons had at least compelled Melinda to get out of the house and do something. Now that she no longer had her weekly lesson, she'd better not get fat. Even if she acted like she hadn't been attracted to Joe for years, he was still into her.

Allen would be here in about ten minutes, having texted Terrence he was just leaving the stable. Terrence had just finished with the girl, so the timing was perfect. He could throw on his breeches and boots like nothing had happened, and she could go brush a horse. She was laying on the sofa like she was in shock, but that was kind of understandable, considering how much he'd just awakened her sexual senses. He highly doubted she'd say a word about their little tryst to anyone, if only because she enjoyed herself so much. He sure as hell did, even if he did most of the "work." That was funny, given the fact she was a "working student."

Following the appointment, Allen told Terrence, "After my rider decides for sure which horse she wants of the two, I'll tell Liam about the one that's still available." They were in the tack room, and Allen's client/rider was outside smoking. (Terrence frowned upon smoking anywhere on his property, but a deal was going through, so he had to make an exception.)

"Him?" Terrence said. "He's got clients who spend lots of money and like imports?"

"Lately he does. He picked up a couple whose families are from Europe. I think one lady's from Germany and the other one's from England, something like that."

Amy Kristoff

"Well hell yeah, let him know, ASAP. I need the money. That and an excuse to cross the pond and pick out some more."

"When do you think you're going again?" Allen wanted to know.

"As soon as possible, like I said. . . Much as I like the latest chick I'm doin', business is business. If she was 'of age,' I'd take her with me."

"You sorry you-know-what. One of these days you are gonna pay for it."

Terrence wasn't sure if Allen was angry, jealous, or just pretending to be either of those, so he said, "I'm not doing anything wrong when it's consensual."

"O.K., whatever, man."

Since Allen didn't sound convinced, Terrence was momentarily worried. However, he didn't dwell on any misgivings; it wasn't his style.

Right then a blue Dodge Caravan pulled up to the barn —the vehicle Monica's father drove. Terrence could see him in the driver's seat, as he had a perfect view of the parking area on the east side of the tack room. Usually Mr. Treble got out and called for his daughter, but today she must have been waiting in the barn doorway because she got right in the passenger side. Allen hadn't really gotten a good look at her until now, as he'd been concentrating on the horses his client was trying.

Allen shook his head, saying, "She's pretty but she can't be more than fifteen . . . and that would be pushing it."

"I don't think she's even close to that . . . oh well." As the minivan departed he added, "Out of sight, out of mind."

Allen shook his head at Terrence but the latter had turned away.

Liam was sore from riding so much today. He not only had yesterday off (Monday) he was getting used to spending more time standing around giving lessons than anything else. He wasn't complaining because the pay was good. One lesson he no longer had to give, however, was for Melinda Treble. Her husband made her quit, no thanks to her bratty daughter. She must have told her pops what his old lady was up to and the guy got jealous. Melinda was determined Liam's ex-girlfriend, Sasha, was the one who'd ratted them out, but how did she get word to Melinda's husband? Liam couldn't help but be obsessed with wondering who told on them. Liam was texting Melinda as much as time would allow. Naturally she was frustrated because he was a lot busier than she was. He was kind of relieved things came to a grinding halt for the time being because he had a feeling all he had to do was say the word and she'd move in with him. The last thing he wanted was a long-term relationship, let alone marriage. Since she currently was married, it was likely she expected the same again, once she finally left her husband.

Here was a text from Allen Snede. He wanted to know if any of Liam's customers might be looking for a super-athletic, bay, Holsteiner gelding, currently at Terrence Stall's.

After texting back, "Maybe. Send some pics," there was a text from Melinda: "Need to see you tonight. I have been allowed some temporary freedom. Name a place. Please!"

The text seemed too good to be true. Liam could cut straight to the chase with Melinda, and if she wasn't good in bed, he'd definitely have no trouble telling her he wasn't interested in a relationship. All he needed to do was think of the perfect place for a rendez-vous.

It occurred to Liam, it was possible the text was part of a trap. Melinda's husband was the one who actually sent it, as he was planning on exacting revenge on Liam, in person. Admittedly Liam had no clue how to defend himself. If Melinda was frustrated with Liam she too might be in on the scheme. The best course of action appeared to be answering the text as if he was indeed communicating with Melinda. If she showed up with her husband, Liam would leave. It sounded simple enough.

Liam decided Melinda and he ought to meet at "The Watering Hole," on Scottsdale Road. There was a spacious patio area in front of the bar/restaurant, and he could watch her approach from the parking area. If he didn't like what he saw/ who he saw her with, he could jump over the three-foot high, decorative block wall that enclosed the patio and make a discreet exit. The bar was part of an inn, behind it. Elegantly decorated suites were discreetly available "on short notice." Rather than ask your waiter what the daily special was, you asked if there was a room. It was very expensive but well-worth the spontaneity. Hopefully the whole idea didn't freak her out, or Liam's plan would backfire.

After Liam texted Melinda where to meet, she took so long to respond he became concerned. She was going to make her husband a cuckold, so she was in possible danger. Finally she agreed to meet there and would see him then. He wasn't certain if it was her.

Liam didn't have to ponder for long because he got the pictures from Terrence Stall. He forwarded them to Anna Criss as well as Madeleine Brecht, two new clients of his who might be interested. What he would have given to make a big commission on selling a horse to either one of those two. He was usually stuck with the cheaper sales, and the buyers typically kept the same horses for years and years.

It was time to grab lunch down the street. The mere thought of making some serious commission money had worked up Liam's appetite. "The Oasis" was the corner café he frequented, which helped break up the day. Nothing was worse than working nonstop.

Right after Liam got his food, he sat on a picnic table out front, and who showed up but his ex-girlfriend, Sasha. He had never before seen her here. Did she only lately begin frequenting this place? He was long past the awkward stage, should he run into her. During any given day, he rarely even saw her from a distance, despite the fact their respective stables were located on the same property. He kept wanting to ask her if she was the one who ratted him and Melinda Treble out.

Sasha appeared a bit surprised to see Liam but did manage to say hi before going in the restaurant to order her food. There was limited indoor seating, so carry-out was a popular option. Even though it was hot outside, Liam had no problem sitting under one of the umbrellas while he ate. Since Sasha was wearing shorts and a T-shirt, hopefully she wouldn't mind sitting out here with him.

Sure enough, she did just that – after asking if it was O.K. Liam was thrilled, actually. She was a pain to live with because she was a neat-freak, but at least she never pressured him to marry her. Melinda Treble made him nervous on that front.

Liam figured he'd point blank ask Sasha what was on his mind: "Are you the one who told Melinda Treble's husband about us maybe appearing too touchy-feely?"

"Come again?"

"Melinda Treble, a former student of mine. Did you ever see us making out for a few seconds and decide to tell her old man on us?"

"I have no idea who or what you're talking about, Liam. Are you trying to make me jealous?"

"No, not at all. I imagine you've moved on by now, although I don't know who you're seeing."

"And I'm not going to tell you."

"Fine with me."

"It sounds like you might be jealous. Ha!"

"Truth be told I'm consumed with wondering who could have told on Melinda and me because her husband would never have known otherwise. I can't seem to think of anything else."

"Sounds to me like you don't have enough to do."

"I have too much, actually. Look at you, dressed for a dune buggy ride, not a horse ride."

Amy Kristoff

"Know what? I got tossed about seven this morning, trying to work a five-year-old, coal black Trakehner gelding that's barely broke. He's too much for his owner, and he must be too much for me, too. She got him through Terrence Stall, who can ride anything and make it look easy. The lady refuses to tell me how much she got taken for. I'm sticking to lessons. I'm a better teacher than a rider, anyway. I'll worry about what to tell her to do with the horse, tomorrow."

"Terrence just sent me some pictures of one he's got left from the last group he bought in Europe. I guess a rider of Al Snede's picked out the second to last one. I'd love to make a nice, big, commission off a sale, so I forwarded the pics to a couple ladies who have the dough. The problem is getting them to spend it on a horse. Both lived abroad at various points in their lives. I always think they're European, but they're originally from here." He wanted to add something about them both being married but too old to seduce, but Sasha would fail to see the humor.

Then Liam had the distinct pleasure of having one of the women he'd sent the pictures to, Anna Criss, text him the following: "When can I try this bay beauty?!! Would it be possible to do it at your place? Could you please arrange that? It would be better for me. THX!!!" He re-read the text because he couldn't believe this money-making opportunity had so easily fallen in his lap. It was impossible Terrence would have a problem with letting Liam borrow the horse in question for a try-out, especially if said horse would be making a one-way trip.

Quickly Liam finished his sandwich, while Sasha was taking her time, clearly in no hurry to return to work. She kept looking at her phone, however. Suddenly she received a text too and after reading it, said, "I don't know if my rider Cynthia's husband answered my prayers or not, but he just showed up at Waverly, grabbed his wife's horse from the stall, loaded it in some tin-can trailer an old geezer was driving and they took off down the road. My new guy Pepe just witnessed the whole damned thing and was afraid to stop him."

"Why should he? Your rider's husband has every right to do whatever the hell he wants with the horse."

"I hope they didn't take him to the killers."

"I wouldn't worry about it if I was you. Now that one won't hurt you."

"I wasn't going to bother trying to ride the horse ever again, anyway. I realized my limits."

"I'm outta here," Liam declared, so excited he could hardly contain himself.

Sasha watched her ex-boyfriend depart, and he appeared completely oblivious to her scrutiny. He still kind of turned her on, but he really had nothing going for him, other than looks and riding ability. She had no idea what she was thinking, having wasted her time living with him. They simply weren't compatible. Nonetheless, he never failed to drop everything to help her if she was having trouble with a horse, unless he was busy giving a lesson. Nowadays she didn't even bother to look in Liam's direction, contrary to whatever his obsession was with being seen making out with some married lady. He was probably secretly proud of as much.

Back at Pinetop, Liam hurriedly backed his pickup truck up to his two-horse trailer, expecting the lights to be working because he had no patience for fiddling around with the wiring. The sooner he could get to Terrence's the better, before another trainer went over there to look. Terrence was actually pretty discerning about who he allowed at his stable because it was on the same property as where he lived. The fact Liam intended to just show up was extremely nervy. Word around the horse world was Terrence liked underage girls, and his occasional advertising for a working student was how he ensnared them.

Liam showed up at Chaparral Jumpers, LLC and parked on the side of the barn. Walking down the aisle way he didn't see anyone, but while passing the closed tack room door he heard someone moaning. After knocking once, Liam opened the door and found Terrence laying on his back, on a sofa, a blue towel over his nose.

Walking over to Terrence, Liam asked him, "You O.K.?"

"No, I'm not. . . I just got hit a couple times, good, by the husband of someone who bought a horse from me. Talk about not appreciating my services."

Liam couldn't help but take advantage of Terrence's temporary vulnerability and brazenly asked if he could "borrow" the horse Terrence was still trying to sell. Terrence told him fine, go ahead, keep the horse overnight if Liam's rider needed more time to decide.

This whole scenario was coming together so perfectly Liam could hardly believe it. The horse was calmer than him when it was loaded in the trailer. That was good because the rider the horse was for, needed a "babysitter." The fact the horse was athletic wasn't the most important aspect. With some of the commission money, Liam was considering taking a vacation. It wasn't too soon to start thinking of where he might want to go, and it never occurred to him he was probably getting ahead of himself.

Terrence honestly wanted no part of allowing Liam Muir to take a pricey sale horse of his to try (or his rider was), but it was obviously the guy's lucky day. It was impossible for Terrence to stand up for himself when he'd just had the crap knocked out of him. Muir was a total loser when it came to having clients with money and aptitude, so he'd probably end up buying "Maple" (the horse's stable name) himself, to save embarrassment. The guy put in the time, however, whether it was riding or giving lessons, so maybe he had the finances. Terrence was terrible at managing money, so he was constantly having to hustle, which was difficult for someone as laid-back as himself.

"Velvet" was the stable name of a horse that was returned

to Terrence without any warning whatsoever, courtesy of the very angry husband who beat up Terrence. The guy had Lou Nettles bring the horse with his shoddy old trailer. The day was coming Terrence would have to install an electronic gate at the end of his driveway, which would help eliminate the possibility of this happening again. Everyone but stupid Liam Muir knew to make an appointment before stopping by. Naturally an irrational husband was another exception to Terrence's unwritten "rule," but a little-known fact was Terrence was irrepressible! That was to say, now that he had Velvet back, including his registration papers, Terrence intended to re-sell him to the next unsuspecting fool. No one asked him for any sort of refund, and he would never provide one, no matter how much he was about to make, selling the horse yet again.

First, Terrence would ride the horse and beat it up (appropriately enough). Once it listened to him, anybody could ride it – for the time being. Before anything, however, he had to get his nose to stop bleeding. He'd try to lay still for a few more minutes.

Liam had a short drive to his stable, but he almost got in an accident! Admittedly he kept glancing at his phone because someone kept texting him. He assumed it was Melinda, anticipating their rendez-vous this evening, but it was Madeleine Brecht, wanting to know if he could find a horse for her to try too! The second Liam reached the driveway leading to Desert Sun Equestrians (where Pinetop Stable was), he pulled over and called Madeleine. She already had the "O.K." from her husband for the "horse money," so she needed Liam to move quickly before her husband changed his mind (came to his senses). Liam tried to tell her she too could try the horse he was bringing now, in case Anna didn't get along with him, but she was adamant that wasn't an option. He couldn't figure out if the two women were best friends or mortal enemies. One thing was clear, however:

they were in competition with one another!

Melinda wanted to warn Liam she might be accompanied by her husband when she showed up at "The Watering Hole" in a couple hours, but she had no way of doing so. It was also possible Joe would drive separately. She was desperate to see Liam and didn't care if she was followed! Hopefully he felt the same way. Joe had finally managed to confiscate her phone and read some texts before they were deleted. Admittedly she'd gotten distracted for a couple minutes, talking to their daughter about her morning at the stable. Ever since Monica had returned she had been in her room, unusual even on a hot summer's day. If she needed to talk about something, Melinda wished she would, versus making Melinda feel guilty for constantly being emotionally unavailable. Maybe getting called out on her flirtations with Liam Muir was a good thing after all; Melinda still wanted to "pursue something" with him, but she had been forced to take stock of the relationship with her daughter, of which Melinda wasn't exactly proud. Monica looked so much more mature than her age, it was easy to forget she was still just a kid and had a lot of growing up to do.

It took longer for Terrence's nose to stop bleeding than it did for him to get Velvet back in line. The horse must have remembered him from the first time around. That was good because Terrence still wasn't feeling too great. The cooling down time for Velvet allowed Terrence to take a breather himself, and he happened to get a phone call. (Terrence was always "connected.") It was none other than Liam Muir! His one rider "fell in love" with Maple and wanted to purchase him without even bothering with a vetting exam, and the other one wanted "whatever Terrence had available sitting around the barn."

Terrence told Liam, "I am sitting on the perfect horse. His stable name is 'Velvet.' He isn't too much for anyone to ride, as long as you keep him tuned up."

"Sure, I can do that."

"Did you say the one buyer is passing on having the horse vetted?"

"She sure is," Liam replied. "And I told her fifty grand for him, not forty-five like you quoted me."

"That'll work for her?"

"As far as I know, and we can split the extra five grand, on top of whatever commission you were going to pay me."

Terrence wanted nothing more than to tell Liam he was a greedy pig and hang up on him. Obviously the guy had never dealt with the likes of Terrence before, who paid the commission he saw fit, at the very end. Often times the exact amount depended on how much of a hassle the buyer and/or trainer ended up being during the transaction. Although this one sounded like it was sailing right through, Muir already pissed Terrence off by holding out his hand, palm straight up. Obviously he was prone to getting ahead of himself. Rather than tell him any of this, however, Terrence said, "Have her make the check out to 'Chaparral Jumpers, LLC.'"

"Sure you don't want her to wire the money? You won't have to worry about a hold on it."

"No, that's O.K. I'm in no hurry," Terrence lied. "Once the check clears I'll hand over the registration papers. Meanwhile she can keep him at your place if you'd like. If not bring him back here."

"He can stay at my place, that's fine," Liam said. Truthfully it wasn't. However, he would look like a cheapskate if he charged either Terrence or the horse's new owner, board. "So what about this 'Velvet' horse you mentioned?"

"He has a little more motor than Maple, but as I mentioned, he should be manageable if you keep after him."

That assessment of Velvet didn't sound as encouraging as the first time the horse was described. Nonetheless, Madeleine Brecht was in full-fledged horse-buying mode and couldn't be swayed, especially if the horse was a real looker.

"What color is he?" Liam asked Terrence, knowing Madeleine preferred a horse that was a slightly unusual color. Therefore, when Terrence replied, "Black," he knew it was probably a done deal. Liam also had a feeling he already knew the horse, albeit indirectly. Hopefully the horse didn't break Madeleine's neck.

Terrence appeared rather unenthusiastic about letting Liam bring Madeleine to Chaparral Jumpers the following morning at nine a.m., to try Velvet. Liam didn't get it. He thought Terrence would have been thrilled to know the troublemaking horse was most likely leaving again soon. Maybe the registration papers were lost in all the confusion, and Terrence figured that would hold up the deal. Liam was certain Madeleine didn't care if the horse was up-to-date with the Trakehner registry. She just wanted a horse that looked impressive. If she ever did some "serious" showing (at rated competitions), Liam would worry about making sure all the paperwork was in order then.

One of Liam Muir's riders was trying Velvet tomorrow at nine a.m., and Terrence should have been ecstatic. Instead, all he could think about was the fact it would cut into his time with Monica, right after her father dropped her off. Terrence wanted to do her and then ride a couple horses before heading to Sedona to visit his sister, Evelyn. She recently moved up there with her husband, Tom, and they were having a get-together. Terrence's invite included staying the night if he cared to. He was thinking of doing so because he needed a break.

Terrence's phone rang again. This time it was Al Snede. Barely had Al said "hello" and he stated, "Dr. Noveno will be there in the morning to vet Laddie."

This was unbelievable. Terrence replied, "Can't Rick come the day after? I have to show a horse to a rider of Liam Muir's and then after I ride some I'm going to my sister's new place in Sedona."

"No problem, I'll reschedule. One more thing . . . Is that horse gonna need some Bute to be sound for all the flexion tests and shit?"

"No, man. That horse is sound as can be. All mine are. I like happy customers, be it horses or humans."

"Great. I'll get that appointment changed and text you the confirmation."

Terrence had to smile. His only problem was a rider who couldn't handle one of his mounts, and her husband took it out on Terrence. This really was a perfect life, overall.

After riding Velvet around the ring a couple more times at a walk, Terrence dismounted. Diego appeared as if out of thin air, to walk the horse back to the barn. Diego knew by now his boss wanted nothing more to do with a horse right after he'd worked it and definitely not this particular one. Diego didn't trust this horse at all and was glad riding wasn't one of his responsibilities.

The last thing Monica wanted to do was tell her mother what Terrence Stall did. It was tempting, however, because maybe she would no longer feel so ambivalent about it. Finally she'd be repulsed and the guy would get in loads of trouble. All Monica wanted was to continue working for him but be left alone. That was probably an impossible request, so she was considering not going to the stable tomorrow, hopefully making him sorry for what he did. She'd think of an excuse in the morning. It was doubtful either of her parents would be curious as to what was really going on.

Given the fact Monica's mother basically had the whole day to text her former trainer and keep the house clean, it wasn't too surprising she appeared slightly more concerned about Monica than she normally did. Monica would still keep her mouth shut about Terrence; she might not believe Monica, anyway. Her mother was obsessed with Liam Muir and only cared about whether he was obsessed with her, too. The only reason Monica's mother didn't drive to his stable to visit was she was paranoid her husband would find out and kill her. Monica knew this for a fact because she overheard him delivering that threat. Monica was pretty sure her father had no idea she heard what she did.

Liam got his "confirmation text" from Al Snede regarding when Laddie would be vetted. Meanwhile, Liam was stopping by Terrence Stall's once last time for the day, to drop off the check for Anna Criss' new horse. Liam expected a receipt or written acknowledgment of the $50,000.00 payment, but Terrence simply folded up the check and put it in his pocket! Liam was certain the guy even smirked at him afterward. Smirked! Maybe Terrence was jealous because Liam looked so dapper. He was on his way to see Melinda Treble and was actually kind of excited. There was nothing to worry about as far as an irate husband, although what happened to Terrence because of a horse was proof it was important to "expect the unexpected." Fortunately Liam knew how to think on his feet, thanks to his decades of training horses.

Where was Liam? That was what Melinda kept asking herself as she walked toward the patio of "The Watering Hole." He was so good-looking Melinda had assumed he would have been easy to see, but there was a sea of faces. It didn't help, she was super-nervous. If Liam stood her up Joe didn't have to worry about killing her because she'd probably kill herself—and she wasn't entirely kidding.
Since Melinda had her phone confiscated before she could confirm 7:30 was an O.K. time to meet, she'd been forced to assume it was acceptable. It was already 7:45, and if Liam treated dates like he did riding lessons, he expected timeliness.
At the same moment Melinda finally saw Liam wave from way in the back of the patio, near the entrance to the restaurant, out of the corner of her left eye she also saw a blue Dodge minivan. She screamed right before getting hit and

ending up on the hood. She then slid back off when the driver slammed on the brakes. Before drifting into unconsciousness, she thought about how sorry she was about everything.

Next of Kin

Real estate was selling so fast in Northwest Indiana, my mother's house on the outskirts of Lowell was under contract in less than a week after it was listed. The buyer didn't care that it was in desperate need of updating and remodeling. Not only that he would be paying full price, cash.

At first this seemed like an enviable situation, as I would be receiving a generous sum for the house at closing. That was despite the fact I would be splitting the amount with my brother, Robert. He had been living with Mom the entire twenty years of his life, but the moment she'd passed he moved in with me. She'd fallen down the stairs leading to the basement. Given the age of the house, the stairway was quite steep. Anyway, the will stated the house had to be sold, the proceeds divided evenly between us. (We were the sole beneficiaries.) Robert had been quite sheltered his whole life and was hardly prepared for home ownership (and was content being basically helpless). I had already completed two years of college when he was born, so I never really knew him. I figured we could enjoy one another's company until Mom's house closed. I had no intention of letting him become a permanent house guest, no matter what he might be expecting. Once he had his share of the money, he was out of here. My space was important to me, although he kept to himself for the most part, playing video games all day.

Meanwhile, the estate was slowly being settled. Other than the house Mom owned free and clear, which had been

It-Girl and Other Stories

in the family for several generations (along with fifty acres of surrounding tillable land that was leased to a farmer), she had few assests. Her possessions were relatively easy to go through because she'd always been very fastidious and didn't collect junk. She always said she didn't want to leave behind a lot of items for "you kids" to throw out because we'd end up hating her. I never thought of it like that and instead wished I was even half as neat as she was. I wasn't a hoarder but I did have a hard time getting rid of something if I thought there was even a remote chance I might need it at some point. I tended to clutter the basement stairway in my house, although at least the stairs weren't difficult to manuveur.

Who was the buyer of Mom's house? I kept wondering as much, and although I knew the person's name, Brent Scarsdale, I didn't know him. My real estate agent, Shaun Bern, was also his agent, so even if he had a fiduciary duty not to tell me any more about the buyer than was necessary, he appeared eager to tell me whatever he could. At least I was prepared for what was going to eventually happen to the property: it would be subdivided into one-acre homesites. Naturally this upset me. I didn't bother apprising Robert of this because he appeared to be in shock over our mother's passing. Fortunately developing the property remained a few years in the future, so I would postpone telling him.

Mr. Scarsdale intended to remodel the house himself. He had a very stressful job and doing remodeling was his way of relaxing. There was no mention from Shaun if Mrs. Scarsdale helped her husband, but she probably did, if only to spend some time with him. Mr. Scarsdale's brother, Jon, was the one who would eventually be subdividing the property, as he was a developer.

The sequence of events began when I stopped in the office of "U-First Realty and Property Management" in downtown Lowell and happened to be greeted by Realtor Shaun Bern when I walked inside. A couple other agents were in there, but he was obviously the most eager. Maybe he needed the business. The extent of my experience with real estate had been purchasing the house I currently owned, close to a dozen years ago. I'd always rented up until that point. My house had been for sale by owner, so I had to do my own negotiating. The seller must have been desperate or it was my lucky day because I got it at a steal.

Once I'd explained my situation to Shaun (I had the O.K. from the attorney handling my mother's estate, to list her property), he was even more enthused to be of service. When he offered to do a "comparative market analysis" to ascertain what the house and land were worth, I told him what it had just been appraised for and he couldn't believe it was so low. I wasn't greedy enough to want top dollar for the property. I wanted this part of my life to be over with so I could move on. It was safe to say my brother wasn't the only one taking our mother's death, hard. At least I thought he was, although I admittedly didn't really know him, as previously mentioned. However, I was aware he was more into technology than I was (and not just video games).

All Shaun had to go on to list the property was the tax records, and he was frustrated about as much, saying, "If your mother's place had been listed before, I would only have to take pictures, and I could copy all the information from the previous listing. I'll have to go out there and measure all the rooms even before I do any picture-taking."

At first I thought the guy was kidding. I would have offered the listing to someone else in the office, but it was probably already too late for that. Leaving would have been the best alternative, but I just stood there. Then, when he indicated for me to follow him to his desk, I did so and proceeded to wait while he downloaded a listing contract for me to sign. He filled out much of it on the computer before printing it. Although I looked it over before adding my signature, I honestly didn't read it thoroughly. About all I noticed was the list price, which he suggested by adding twenty grand to the appraisal, having made no more mention of doing a comparative market analysis. Maybe he already forgot about it.

I didn't think there was anything "wrong" with Shaun not even looking at the property before having me sign the listing contract (and he did so, as well). As mentioned I knew nothing about real estate transactions. He did, however, want a key so he could put the house on a "lockbox." He asked me if the house really was vacant, having already told him it was. He said it was "more inviting for showings if it was vacant." I thought that was a cruel remark, unintended though its cruelty probably was. In other words the house was vacant because the owner was dead!

It occurred to me (albeit briefly) I could try to sell the house myself, despite the fact I'd know nothing about what I was doing. I figured I could tear up the listing contract I'd just signed and Shaun would be O.K. with it. Maybe he sensed I was having reservations about him because he reassured me, saying, "I will keep you in the loop about what's going on."

When I got home it was time to start thinking about dinner, and I figured updating Robert on the latest developments with Mom's house would go over better when everyone had a full stomach. I'd made my specialty, chicken noodle soup, earlier, and all I had to do was heat it up. One compliment Robert had paid me that was very flattering: I was a better cook than Mom. I appreciated that because he didn't have to bother to say it, as he wasn't much for conversation, I was finding out. Admittedly Mom never was an exceptional cook, but she was definitely above-average, if only in her willingness to try new recipes.

I hadn't even served the two of us when my cell phone rang and it was Shaun. He had this to shout: "You're never going to believe it! I already have someone who wants to see your lisiting! I barely got the pictures uploaded on the computer and someone stopped in the office, just like you did earlier!"

At the time I'd thought it sounded a little too coincidental, but I was willing to accept anything I was told (partially due to the grief mindset). It never occurred to me to look up the listing online, to confirm it even existed. Doing so would have required too much technological effort, and I didn't want to bother Robert about it. I ended up telling him who had called and that things were moving "very quickly" getting the house sold. He nodded but looked more sullen than usual. I hurried to finish getting dinner on the table.

Anyway, that first showing led to the full-price, cash offer. Even someone like me knew to accept it. Not only that, the buyer was willing to forgo any pre-purchase inspections. In turn, Shaun had remarked, "Be happy about that, since you have well water!" Again, I couldn't figure out if he was kidding. He had to be, didn't he? Maybe I simply didn't "get" his sense of humor. I knew one thing: I was already sick and tired of how "funny" he evidently considered himself. Luckily there didn't seem to be any hurdles to getting the house sold. Like my house, the basement never flooded, although mine was in a flood zone.

Supposedly Shaun had submitted the purchase agreement to Landon Field, the attorney for my mother's estate, who in turn would give it to the probate judge for final approval.

I didn't consider it unusual that several days passed and I hadn't heard anything from Attorney Field, regarding the purchase agreement. Meanwhile, Shaun had mentioned depositing the thousand-dollar earnest money check in his personal checking account because he didn't trust leaving the money in the U-First Realty account designated for as much. His excuse sounded reasonable, so I didn't think any more about it. I was more concerned with the forecast of an inch of rain. With my luck, the basement in Mom's house would flood, despite never having done so. I wanted the deal to hurry up and close! It had been a dry summer, so it seemed figurable mid-September would be rainy.

After a few more days, I became impatient and called Shaun, wanting to know if I could somehow obtain a copy of the signed purchase agreement. I didn't even bother to ask if Attorney Field finally received a copy and ASSUMED he did.

Sounding nervous, Shaun said, "I know you don't have a printer and even faxing something to you is out of the question, so how about you stop by the office later?"

I told him I would be there a little after three o'clock. I figured if I told him what time, he would make sure to be there. Since I was a client of his, wouldn't he want to personally hand me the paperwork? Just because I hated technology was no reason for Shaun to be dismissive of me.

Usually I got off work at three, as I started at six-thirty and had a half-hour lunch break. (I was a caregiver at "Sunset Haven" on Main Street in Lowell.) On this particular day, Gladys Johnstone went into cardiac arrest at two-fifty and an ambulance was called. Then it started raining. At exactly three it still hadn't arrived but the dispatcher was on the line, reassuring Sunset Haven's supervisor, Kathy Mintz, help was on the way. Gladys was ninety-one, so it was possible her final moments were upon her. Kathy did not want Gladys to die at the senior care facility. On the ambulance ride to the hospital or at the hospital itself were the places Kathy preferred. In the meantime, I was not allowed to leave until Gladys was on her way – in the physical sense. I had worked here for several years and no one had ever passed away on my shift. I wanted the record to remain intact. Admittedly, there was no humor in my attitude at the time, as my mother's sudden, unexpected passing had put things in perspective.

U-First Realty's office wasn't more than a three-minute drive from Sunset Haven but might as well have been an hour away. It didn't take the ambulance driver quite that long to show up, but I was starting to wonder if the paramedics had the same dilemma as Kathy, not wanting a body to deal with. Meanwhile, a family member of Gladys' had been notified of the situation.

Finally I was able to depart for U-First Realty. This time I had to park in a large, paved parking lot that was shared by a number of businesses, rather than parallel- park in front of the building. When I tried the door it was locked. I'd gotten soaking wet for nothing. I didn't have my cell phone with me, to attempt to contact Shaun. I would go home to call Attorney Field, to find out if he ever received the purchase agreement. I ASSUMED I would be able to get the truth out of the latter.

Back home, Robert appeared to be in "his" room, which was across from mine. Most likely he was doing what else but playing a video game. It was a three-bedroom, one-bath, ranch-style house that wasn't spacious but definitely roomy enough for one person. Albeit unfinished, the full basement provided plenty of space for storage. Also, the third bedroom was filled with stuff. Robert was lucky I'd bothered to have a spare bedroom. Given the hurry he'd been in to leave Mom's following her unfortunate fall, I was never sure if he left because he was afraid to be alone or he was "behind" her fatal tumble.

Even before changing into some dry clothes, I had to check the basement, making sure it wasn't finally flooding. That was my last thought before I was pushed down the stairs, hard. Since they weren't nearly as steep and treacherous as the ones in Mom's house, I was just banged up. Or maybe I got lucky.

There was no water in the basement, but something was trickling down my forehead. Wiping it away, I realized it was blood. At least I knew how Mom fell, after all.

About the Author

Amy has written several novels and short story collections, including a trio of books with off-beat dog themes. She lives on a horse farm in Indiana. AmyKristoff.com.